DRAGON DETECTIVE

SKY HIGH!

GARETH P. JONES

For my brother, Adam – G.J.

STRIPES PUBLISHING LIMITED
An imprint of the Little Tiger Group
1 Coda Studios, 189 Munster Road,
London SW6 6AW

www.littletiger.co.uk

A paperback original
Originally published in Great Britain under the title
The Case of the Vanished Sea Dragon by Bloomsbury Publishing Plc in 2008
Text copyright © Gareth P. Jones, 2008, 2020
Illustration copyright © Scott Brown, 2020
Author photograph © David Boni
Additional images used under licence from Shutterstock.com

ISBN: 978-1-78895-175-3

The Forest Stewardship Council® (FSC®) is a global, not-for-profit organization
dedicated to the promotion of responsible forest management worldwide. FSC defines
standards based on agreed principles for responsible forest stewardship that are supported
by environmental, social, and economic stakeholders. To learn more, visit www.fsc.org

10 9 8 7 6 5 4 3 2 1

DRAGON DETECTIVE
SKY HIGH!

GARETH P. JONES

LITTLE TIGER
LONDON

The double-chinned security guard sat slumped in front of a wall of black-and-white TV screens. He opened his bleary eyes, yawned and pulled a doughnut from the box. He took a bite, licking a globule of jam that dribbled down his chin, unaware that every move he made was being watched by a four-metre-long, red-backed, green-bellied, urban-based Mountain Dragon, who was perfectly blended with the sloping rooftop across the road.

Dirk Dilly, dragon detective, gazed longingly at the doughnuts. He was starving. To take his mind off his rumbling stomach he opened his book and read.

"Now, where was I?" he muttered.

Dragon Births

A pregnant female dragon will travel deep into the earth's belly to the banks of the Outer Core, where she lays the egg. She then picks it up in her mouth and dives into the liquid fire. This is an extremely painful experience. The mother plants the egg in the liquid fire and returns to the shore, where she waits for her youngling to hatch and swim to the surface.

Dirk examined an illustration of dragons waiting for their newborn babies to appear from the bubbling underground lake.

A female Sea Dragon places her egg relatively near the surface of the fiery lake, giving its offspring's skin the ability to soften in water. A Mountain Dragon's egg is planted deeper into the lava, making the child's back tougher and giving it the chameleon-like ability to blend with its environment. It is the Sky Dragon that buries its egg deepest. It takes weeks for a young Skyling to swim to the surface, by which time the fire has

become a permanent part of its composition. This
gives it the rare power known as 'sublimation', the
ability to turn its entire body into cloud-like gas.

Dirk looked up from the book. Nothing had changed. The screens still showed the interior of an art gallery located above a doughnut shop on a busy London street. At night, the doors were locked but they might as well have stayed locked during the days for all the visitors the gallery got.

Dirk had been watching the gallery every night since he got the call from a plummy-voiced man who had introduced himself as Mr Strettingdon-Smythe, the curator.

"Important pieces are going missing," Mr Strettingdon-Smythe said over the phone.

"Don't you have security?" Dirk had held the receiver between his shoulder and his long, pointy ear as he reached for his glass of neat orange squash.

"Yes, but he's useless – always asleep on the job."

"Why don't you fire him?" asked Dirk, draining the contents of the glass.

"I wish I could but he's a relative of the owner."

"What about CCTV?"

"Every room is monitored but the picture goes fuzzy whenever a painting goes missing, like it's being interfered with somehow."

"Why don't you go to the police?" Dirk had enquired.

"The owner says it's bad for business. Although I can't see how business could be any worse," the curator replied bitterly.

Mr Strettingdon-Smythe explained that there had been four thefts so far, each following the same pattern. Late at night the CCTV would go haywire for around an hour, during which time the thieves somehow removed a painting without breaking any windows, setting off the alarmed door or showing signs of forced entry. In each case the broken frame was left behind. Only the picture itself was taken.

It sounded intriguing. Dirk agreed to take on the case.

"And, Mr Dilly," added Mr Strettingdon-Smythe, "I'd appreciate utmost discretion. I haven't told the owner I hired you. I know he would disapprove but

I can't bear to have any more pieces go missing. Please don't let anyone see you."

"Believe me, it would be a bigger problem for me than for you if I was seen."

Dirk's first thought was that it had to be an inside job. The obvious suspect was the double-chinned security guard but, after a few days following him, Dirk uncovered no signs of guilt. During the day, the man worked on the security desk of an office building. He had a cheery nature and enjoyed greeting every employee by name. After a full day's work, he headed to the art gallery, via the doughnut shop, and spent the evening stuffing his face and dozing off. He was incompetent and sleep deprived but he wasn't corrupt.

The question that bothered Dirk was why the thieves didn't take the whole lot in one go. Why take one painting at a time, risking capture with each return visit? It didn't make any sense and, after almost two weeks staking out the gallery, Dirk was no closer to getting any answers.

He opened his book and flicked to a page on Sky Dragons.

If you have ever looked up at a cloud in the shape of a dragon, the chances are you have seen a Sky Dragon.

Since dragonkind went into hiding it is generally believed that all of the world's Sky Dragons have remained in a 'sublimated' gas-like state. Some say their return will signify the beginning of the great war between dragons and humans but, in truth, no one knows.

If a Sky Dragon were to materialize, it would leave a dragon-shaped trace of ash on the ground. The process of changing from solid matter into a gas state and vice versa is thought to be very painful. Some claim they can distil water from the clouds and create powerful firewalls but, as with so much about this rare species, no one knows for sure.

The book, *Dragonlore*, had been written by Ivor Klingerflim, the late husband of Dirk's landlady. It worried Dirk that a human could know so much about dragons. There was a chapter on eating habits, which correctly identified all dragons as vegetarians, and sections on how different types of dragon varied in appearance, strength and powers. It was spot-on in every detail. It even covered types of dragon he had never encountered, such as the Californian Desert Dragons who apparently had spikes sticking out of their backs and spat poison instead of breathing fire.

He had no idea how Ivor had learned so much, but he was relieved when Mrs Klingerflim had said that he could only afford to print a hundred copies.

"He spent his whole life studying dragons," she had explained.

"So weren't you surprised when you discovered that I was one?" Dirk had asked, feeling foolish, always having assumed that Mrs Klingerflim's poor eyesight was the reason that she didn't scream when she first saw him.

"Very little surprises you when you get to my age," the old lady had replied. "Except for ice cream."

"Ice cream?"

"Oh yes, all the new flavours they keep bringing out. I bought a tub of salted caramel the other day. Goodness me. Caramel with salt. Whatever next? Sugary asparagus sorbet? I wouldn't be surprised."

Dirk often found himself replaying conversations

with Mrs Klingerfilm on slow days and, since taking the art gallery case, there had been a lot of those.

The double-chinned security guard fell asleep, dropping the half-eaten doughnut on to the floor. Dirk was about to return to his book when he noticed the CCTV screens flicker and the picture disappear.

He checked the street below. At the bus stop a few late-night party-goers were waiting for the night bus home, eating revolting-looking kebabs and dripping chilli sauce on the pavement. None of them looked up. Londoners rarely did.

He flew to the large window and peered inside the gallery. There was no sign of a break-in but, on the far wall, a painting of a sad-looking lady had fallen to the floor, shattering the glass.

Dirk pushed his nose to the window and saw the picture lift itself out of the frame and move across the floor.

He pushed the window open and entered the gallery. It was risky but he knew the CCTV cameras would still be down. Standing on his hind legs, he surveyed the scene. No sign of anyone. In one corner of the room was a small red light. He bent down and inspected it. The light was coming from a black sphere about the size of a golf ball. Dirk picked it up. He had seen similar devices before. They gave off a small electromagnetic pulse, knocking out all electronic devices in their vicinity.

"That explains the cameras," he said to himself.

He tucked the black sphere behind his wing and noticed a second blinking light on a white box attached to the ceiling. Realizing what it was, he clamped his paw over his nostrils. But it was too late to stop the thin line of grey smoke drifting up from his nose through the room into a vent in the small box. Dirk knew exactly what would happen next. The smoke particles would neutralize the ions, causing a drop in current between the two plates in the ionization chamber, triggering the smoke alarm.

"Rats," he muttered, as the sound filled the room. Case or no case, he couldn't afford to be seen by a human. He dived back out of the window just in time as the double-chinned security guard entered the room, holding a fire extinguisher. He didn't spot the painting moving across the floor until he tripped over it. As he fell, he pulled the pin out of the extinguisher, spraying foam everywhere.

From his position on the roof across the road, Dirk could see that the security cameras had come back on and were recording the farcical scene inside the gallery from various angles. He was relieved he had got out in time. To be seen by a human was to breach the forbidden divide between dragonkind and mankind. Mrs Klingerflim and Holly were human, of course, but that was different. Mrs K and Holly were his friends.

There had been much change in the Bigsby household following Mrs Bigsby's defeat in the general election. The morning after, there had been tears and consolation – although neither came from Holly. The following week there were angry phone calls and arguments.

Following this very public loss, Holly had found herself feeling uncharacteristically sorry for her stepmum as she moped miserably about the house. Mrs Bigsby had never spent so much time at home.

It was surprising then, when, on the final day of the summer term, Holly returned home to discover her stepmother in the kitchen, smartly dressed, carefully arranging delicate morsels of food on a plate.

"What's going on?" asked Holly.

"We have a very important guest coming tonight," replied Mrs Bigsby. "So I need you on your best behaviour."

A small, furry white face with a black smudge on its nose followed Holly into the kitchen.

"And keep that animal away from my canapés," said Mrs Bigsby.

Holly picked up Willow and nuzzled her.

"What guest?" she asked. "Dad said we'd have pizza because it's my last day of school for the summer."

"You can have pizza in your bedroom. Brant Buchanan is visiting."

"Who's Brant Buchanan?" asked Holly.

"*Who's Brant Buchanan?*" squawked her stepmum incredulously. "He's the seventh richest man in the world, that's who. He runs Global Sands."

Holly shrugged. "Never heard of it. What do they do?"

"Look him up online if you're so interested." Mrs Bigsby picked up the tray and carried it through to the living room.

Her dad entered the kitchen. "Hi, Holly. How was school?"

"Great. It's been cancelled." She paused before adding, "For six weeks anyway."

Mr Bigsby smiled. "I know you've been struggling to fit in but you'll find your people, I'm sure," he said. "Gristle Street Comprehensive must be quite a contrast to your last school."

"Who's this special guest then?" asked Holly, changing the subject.

"He's a businessman. Your mother is hoping to get a job out of it."

"Stepmother," Holly corrected. "A job doing what?"

"Getting paid," he said, raising his eyebrows, "and given that a billionaire is popping in for tea, potentially getting paid rather a lot."

"It's no wonder that everyone at school thinks I'm posh, is it?"

"Is that boy still bullying you? What's his name? Archie something?"

"No. I'm fine."

That boy's name was Archie Snellgrove. Over the last term, he had teased Holly mercilessly. At first, he just called her posh. When he learned that her previous school had been William Scrivener, school for the children of the rich and famous, he had repeatedly asked her for an autograph. More recently, Mrs Bigsby's failed election campaign had been the target of his jibes.

In a moment of weakness, Holly had admitted this to her dad. She had regretted it ever since. Holly preferred to deal with her own problems.

"Now, you had better make yourself scarce," said Mr Bigsby. "This means a lot to your … to Angela. Since losing her seat… Well, you know what she's been like. A job like this would really help her confidence, not to mention our ability to pay for this house."

Holly went to her room where she changed out of her school uniform and switched on her computer. Willow occupied herself chasing a fly around, while Holly typed 'Global Sands' into the search engine and found the official website. A dark blue G and S in a circle materialized on the screen, then the home page appeared. It showed all the different things that the company did. The website had links to other divisions of the company too: GS Automobiles, GS Homes,

GS Telecoms, GS Air, GS Records, GS Solutions, all linked by the same logo.

She went back to the search results and found a recent news article with a picture of a silver-haired man.

A series of protests are being organized in London by animal rights activists targeting multi-billionaire Brant Buchanan whose multinational company, Global Sands, is accused of engaging in cruel animal experimentation.

Mr Buchanan, founder of Global Sands (and seventh richest man in the world), dismissed the allegations as 'ill informed'.

Holly scrolled through some of the other articles. There were lots of boring business stories about Buchanan buying and insuring islands and something about his plans to purchase a large insurance company, but Holly was more interested in reading about the allegations of animal cruelty. She followed links to sites speculating on what experiments Global Sands was involved in. It was horrible. Willow meowed at

Holly's ankle and Holly picked her up.

As she scrolled through the images, a motor engine stopped outside the house. Holly looked through the window and saw an extremely expensive silver car. The driver, dressed entirely in grey, leaped out and opened the back door in one smooth movement. A silver-haired man in a black suit emerged from the car and strode up to Holly's front door.

The doorbell rang. Holly looked back at the pictures on the computer screen. Mrs Bigsby answered the door. "Mr Buchanan, it's such a great pleasure. Please come in."

"Thank you," replied the visitor. "Please, call me Brant."

3

Dirk was on the familiar route back to his office, jumping from rooftop to rooftop. He somersaulted on to a school building and dived off the edge, spreading his wings, gliding down to a row of houses and running across them, over a busy road, checking the street below before soaring through the open window.

It was such a familiar route that he could have done it blindfolded. It came as a surprise then, when he crashed headfirst into something inside his office.

"Owmph!" he exclaimed as the rest of his body caught up with his face.

Whatever Dirk had hit was scaly, unstable and moving backwards. He knocked the light switch with the tip of his tail and saw that he was face to face with a rather startled-looking Sea Dragon, who was foaming at the mouth and staggering precariously through his office.

Dirk wasn't exactly the tidiest of dragons. Old newspapers, case files, discarded orange-squash bottles and empty baked bean tins littered the floor. The Sea Dragon tripped and lost its footing, sending Dirk flying over its head.

Dirk collided with his filing cabinet, which rocked back, knocking the television that had been resting on top.

"Oof." The flat screen landed on Dirk's head and he had to quickly grab it to prevent it from bouncing off and smashing on the floor. He placed it carefully back. It was unharmed, which was more than he could say for himself.

He rubbed his head. He couldn't see the other dragon any more but there was only one place in his office big enough for a dragon to hide. Under his desk. It was the largest desk he had been able to find online but it was still a bit of a squeeze to get under. Dirk knew how the Sea Dragon was feeling.

The pins and needles would have started and soon the cramp would follow.

"Hello, Mr Dilly," called Mrs Klingerflim from the landing. "Is everything all right in there?"

"Fine, Mrs K," responded Dirk. "Just clumsy old me."

"Right-o. Call if you want anything. I'll be putting the kettle on in a minute. A man at the station gave me a free sachet of herbal tea. I don't usually like herbal things but I do like a freebie … and 'sachet' is such a fun word to say. So we'll have to see how it tastes."

"OK," said Dirk. "Thanks, Mrs K."

Dirk dropped on to all fours and approached the desk. He picked up a bottle of orange squash and poured himself a glass.

"Whoever you are," he said, "you shouldn't be here. You know the punishment for breaching the forbidden divide."

"Of course, I know," said the other dragon. "But it is not me who is living in this human hive. Our kind are supposed to stay hidden."

Dirk shrugged. He knew the risks. Ever since

19

a conference held high in the Himalayas around a thousand years ago, the dragon world had gone into hiding. Those in favour of fighting had risen into the air and became known as up-airers. Minertia, the greatest dragon of all, had counted the votes and announced the result. Attacking a human, being seen by a human or allowing a human to find evidence of dragons were outlawed. Many dragons were banished to the Inner Core as a consequence, including Minertia herself.

"OK, here's what I know about you," said Dirk. "You're a Sea Dragon who recently left the sea in a hurry and travelled to London specifically to find me. You haven't eaten in a while and you have never had any dealings with humans before."

The desk wobbled and the Sea Dragon's head appeared.

"How are you knowing all these facts?" she said. It was a female, with some kind of accent. Dirk wasn't sure what, maybe Spanish.

"Well, it's not difficult to see you're a Sea Dragon. The gills are a dead give-away. A Sea Dragon's back hardens with time out of water, but your back is still soft. Usually you would hide out until it hardens but you didn't, so that means you were in a hurry. You're under my desk so you came looking for me." Dirk blew a smoke ring. "How did I do?"

"How did you know about the food?"

Dirk pointed to the dragon's foaming mouth. "Only a hungry dragon would steal food from my office and only one who doesn't know much about humans would eat a bar of soap."

"I did not like it," replied the Sea Dragon, spitting out bubbles. "Not one bit."

"So, what brings you to London?" asked Dirk.

The Sea Dragon climbed out from under the desk and cricked her back. "I am wanting the help from you."

"What sort of help?"

"Detective help," she replied, "like you give the humanos. My name is Alba Longs. My sister, Delfina, has gone vamoosed. We meet up every year in the same place, in the mountains of Spain, but she was not there this time and I am needing you to help finding her."

"I don't take cases from dragons," replied Dirk.

"They're too much trouble and they don't pay well."

"I can pay," she said. "I have gold."

Dirk smiled. "Gold's great in the dragon world but I can't exactly pay the rent with it or use it to tip the pizza delivery guy, can I?"

Alba looked confused. "I do not know who the rent is or what the … pizza delivery guy … might be, but you must help me. I have no one else to be asking."

"Do I look like I give a rat's banjo? You shouldn't be this close to humans. It's not safe."

"But *you* are living with them and speaking with them and making work with them. Please. I must find my sister."

Alba was prowling around the room, inspecting the strange objects she found on the floor. She picked up an unopened tin of chilli-flavoured baked beans. "What is this?" she asked.

"My dinner," replied Dirk tersely.

"Food? Oh, please!" she begged.

"Fine. Have some beans, then go."

Alba bit into the can, sending beans and chilli tomato sauce across the room, splattering the walls and catching Dirk in the eye. Red gloop dribbled down her chin as she chewed, crushing the metal between her jaws before gulping it down.

"I very like it," she said, burping. "But the shell is quite crunchy."

Dirk wiped the sauce off his face.

"Oh, what is this?" she asked, picking up the TV remote control.

"Leave my stuff alone," barked Dirk. "I've told you, I can't help you find—"

Dirk's words were drowned out by the TV, which Alba managed to turn on. A group of scruffy looking teenagers were playing guitars and screaming, "*We're louder than a juggernaut, we're crazy like a fox, we're playing our guitars and not wearing any socks.*"

Petrified by the noise, Alba threw the remote control behind her and ran at the TV. Dirk tried to block her but she whacked him in the ear and leapfrogged over him.

"Stop the loudness!" she screamed, knocking the TV off the filing cabinet once again. Dirk attempted to catch it but Alba was in his way and he watched helplessly as this time it smashed. The screen went blank but the speakers were unaffected and the rock band continued to sing.

"*We do whatever we want, beg, steal or borrow. We were rocking all of yesterday and we'll carry on tomorrow. Yeah.*"

"The loudness… Make the loudness stop!" yelled Alba.

A pounding came on the door.

"Mr Dilly, are you all right?" It was Mrs Klingerflim.

"Fine, Mrs K. Sorry, it's my TV," he replied.

"Well, it's quite noisy, dear."

"Yes, I'll turn it down," replied Dirk.

"*Fish will swim, birds will fly, I'll keep rocking till I—*"

Another banging started, this one from the adjacent wall. A voice shouted, "Keep the bleeding noise down or I'll call the bleeding police!"

BANG BANG.

"Make the loudness stop!"

BANG BANG BANG.

"*We don't care what our parents say, they're far too old and sad.*"

BANG BANG BANG BANG.

"The loudness!"

"We just wanna rock all day, so leave it out, Mum and Dad."

BANG   BANG   BANG   BANG BANG.

"Stop the loudness!"

"Yeah, yeah, yeah, we wanna rock."

"Oi! You're disturbing the bleeding peace."

"Mr Dilly, the neighbours are complaining."

BANG BANG BANG BANG BANG BANG.

Dirk's head felt like it was going to cave in and just when he thought it couldn't get any louder, the phone started to ring.

4

Holly could hear her stepmum downstairs, loudly fawning over her guest. "Tell me, Brant, do you really own three islands?"

"Four, actually. It sounds impressive but if you could see them, they're just lumps of rock."

Mrs Bigsby laughed annoyingly. Holly could think of nothing worse than joining them but the smell of food proved too tempting for Willow. She wriggled out of Holly's arms and ran downstairs.

"Willow," whispered Holly. "Willow!"

The cat ignored her and slipped into the front room.

"Get away, you awful thing," squawked Mrs Bigsby.

Holly darted down the stairs and burst into the room.

"Leave her alone," she said.

Mrs Bigsby was shooing Willow away with her foot. Mr Buchanan stood by the fireplace. Up close, he looked older than in the photograph on the website. And the picture hadn't done justice to his penetrating grey-green eyes, which descended upon Holly. She felt herself take a step backwards, as though his gaze was too intense to stand so close. She knocked a table behind her and a glass fell and smashed on the wooden floor. Willow jumped out of the way.

"I must apologize, Mr Buchanan," said Mrs Bigsby. "The creature isn't house-trained."

Holly didn't know whether her stepmum was referring to the cat or to her.

"I'm sorry." Holly kneeled down to pick up the shards.

"Leave it." Mrs Bigsby grabbed her hand, accidentally causing the sharp piece of glass that Holly had been carefully holding with her fingertips to slip. The edge was so fine that Holly didn't feel it cut into her skin until she saw the red slash across her palm.

"Holly, you've cut yourself." Mrs Bigsby sounded more annoyed than concerned.

Mr Buchanan, who had been watching with an air of detachment, seemed suddenly interested at the sight of blood. He leaned forwards. "That will take some time to heal," he said.

The fine red line thickened as blood oozed out. The sight made Holly feel faint. The pain was beginning to register.

"Don't drip on the furniture," squawked Mrs Bigsby, grabbing a bowl from the sideboard and handing it to Holly. "Hold this under it."

Holly took the bowl in time to catch the first droplet of blood.

"Does it hurt?" Mr Buchanan asked.

"A little, yes," she replied.

"Pain helps us understand our limitations. Only by experiencing such extremes can we learn more about ourselves."

"Is that why you hurt innocent animals?" said Holly angrily.

Mr Buchanan smiled and picked up Willow who was purring by his feet. "I believe animals are far more intelligent than we give them credit for," he said. "See your cat, for instance. She didn't cut herself on the broken glass."

"I heard a crash." Holly's dad entered the room and looked at his daughter. "What's happened? Come on, we'd better find a plaster. I'm so sorry, Mr Buchanan."

"There's really no need," said the billionaire. "I require a moment alone with your wife anyway."

Holly followed her father through to the kitchen, where he located a first-aid kit.

"It looks like quite a cut. Perhaps I should take you to hospital." He wrapped a bandage around her hand.

"It's fine," said Holly hastily.

The wound would heal as she slept. Self-healing skin was one of the dragon powers she had gained from consuming a small amount of Dirk's blood, but that was hardly the sort of thing she could tell her father.

"Now, please try not to, you know, get in the way," he said. "If your mother gets this job, it could make a big difference to us."

"She shouldn't work for a man who hurts animals," said Holly stubbornly.

"Life's more complicated when you're a grown up," replied her dad.

"It's not exactly simple when you're young," replied Holly.

"I suppose not," he admitted.

With her hand bandaged, she left the kitchen and walked loudly upstairs only to tiptoe quietly back down again. She could hear low murmuring from the living room. She crept back to the door and, ever so gently, eased it open. Seeing an opportunity, Willow darted inside.

"That cat!" snarled Mrs Bigsby.

Holly used the distraction to slide into the room. She pushed herself against a wall and vanished from sight as she turned exactly the same floral pattern as the wallpaper. Blending was another power she had picked up from the dragon blood.

Neither Mrs Bigsby nor Brant Buchanan noticed her enter. Mrs Bigsby picked up Willow, carried her to the door and flung her out. She closed the door behind her.

"She's persistent, I'll give her that," said Mr Buchanan. "What's her name?"

"Er…" Mrs Bigsby thought for a moment. "Pillow? Something like that. She belongs to the child."

"Children need company," replied Mr Buchanan. "She's very strong-willed, isn't she?"

"The cat?"

"Your daughter."

"*Step*daughter. And yes."

Holly was concentrating hard on remaining still. Mr Buchanan glanced at the patch of wall where she was hiding. She closed her eyes.

"Anyway, to the matter in hand," he said.

Holly opened one eye to see him walk across the room, but he didn't sit down, instead putting his palms outstretched on the table.

"Can you help me, Angela?" he said, fixing her with a firm gaze.

"I'm sorry. I honestly can't see how I can. I lost my job. The other lot deal with it now."

"Yes, but we both know how these things work. Little will have changed. They haven't scrapped the AOG project. All I need is the location."

Holly felt her heartbeat quicken. The AOG project was a secret government scheme. AOG stood for

Acts of God and referred to weapons designed to create natural disasters. She knew this because she had helped Dirk stop a rebel group of dragons known as the Kinghorns from using an earthquake creator called the QC3000 to wipe out half of Europe.

"I wouldn't want to be involved in anything, well... I've always been very above board..." Holly had never heard her stepmum sound so nervous.

"Oh, don't worry. I'm the chairman of the board," replied Mr Buchanan, chuckling at his own joke. "Your future at Global Sands will be both secure and bright. Above all, we reward loyalty."

"Can I think about it?"

Mr Buchanan turned and took a couple of steps towards the door. Holly saw him bite his lip in frustration before putting on a smile and turning around.

"Of course you can," he said. "But please remember I have spoken to you in confidence."

"Yes, I understand and I'm grateful. I know how valuable your time is."

"Valuable and expensive," replied Mr Buchanan, inspecting a mini fishcake before thinking better of it and placing it back on the tray.

"Should I call you?" asked Mrs Bigsby.

"No, I'll call you tomorrow. Please don't disappoint me, Angela. I loathe being disappointed."

Mr Buchanan opened the door and left. Holly heard the front door close, then Mr Bigbsy came back into the room.

"Well? What did he say? Did he offer you a position?" he asked.

"Yes."

Holly couldn't see her stepmum's face but her dad didn't look as pleased with this news as she had expected. Mrs Bigsby must have noticed this too.

"I have to take it," she said.

"Have to?" asked her dad, with a raised eyebrow.

"It's too good an opportunity to refuse."

Holly missed the rest of the conversation because they walked out but as soon as she knew it was safe, she picked up the phone and dialled Dirk's number.

Dirk yanked the television plug out of the socket with his tail. The sound cut out, the banging from next door ceased, Mrs Klingerflim went quiet and Alba stopped screaming. He picked up the ringing phone.

"The Dragon Detective Agency," he said, catching his breath. "Dirk Dilly speaking. How can I help you?"

"It's me..."

It was Holly's voice, but he couldn't hear what she said next because Alba spoke over her, saying, "I have been telling you already. I want you to help finding my sister."

"I'm not speaking to you," Dirk said to Alba, causing the Sea Dragon to lower her head apologetically.

34

"What have I done?" said Holly, thinking he meant her.

"Not you," replied Dirk.

"Then you will help me?" said Alba.

"Dirk, I need your help," said Holly.

"No, I won't help you," replied Dirk, again speaking to Alba.

"Why? What's wrong?" said Holly.

"You are very indecisive," said Alba.

"Look, can I call you back?" he said into the phone, turning away from Alba.

"What's going on?" asked Holly.

"Why do you want to call me *Back*?" asked Alba. "My name is Alba."

"Nothing. I'll call you back," said Dirk, hanging up.

"OK, I let you call me *Back* if you promise to help me," said the Sea Dragon.

"Haven't you ever heard of a phone?" asked Dirk.

"A-forrn," repeated Alba. "I have not heard of A-forrn. Is this another of your crunchy-shelled humano food stuffs?"

"Never mind. You have to go." Dirk picked up the broken TV and placed it back on the filing cabinet.

"You've caused enough damage for one day."

"But I will not go without you," she replied. "I need your help. I need the help of the great Mr Dirk Dilly, dragon detective."

"How do you know about me anyway?" asked Dirk, his eyes narrowing. "How do you know where I live?"

"The Shade-Hugger said not to say— Oops!" she said, clasping a paw to her mouth.

"What Shade—" Dirk stopped mid-sentence. "Karny."

"Captain Karnataka," Alba corrected him.

Dirk sighed. His old friend Karnataka was the most corrupt dragon he had ever met. He was a swindler, a con-artist and a thief. His most daring feat had been to steal the Council's Welsh gold reserves from under their noses, so it was ironic that the Council had since seen fit to elect him captain of the Dragnet, the dragon police force.

The question that bothered Dirk right now was why Karnataka would pass on his details to this Sea Dragon.

"I can't help you," he said. "I've already got a case on the go."

"But if I do not find my sister, I do not know what I will do…" Alba broke off and burst into a howling wail.

The banging from next door started again.

"Oi, stop that bleeding racket before I come round and give you an extreme close-up of my fist!" yelled the neighbour.

"Mr Dilly, the neighbours are complaining again!" shouted Mrs Klingerflim.

"All right," Dirk said through gritted teeth. "I don't seem to have any choice but to help you."

Alba stopped making the noise.

"Are you talking to me or Aforrn … or whoever Back is?"

"You."

"So you will help me find my sister?"

Of all the bad ideas he'd had in his life, helping Alba was the worst. It was even worse than the time he decided to mix his favourite foods together – the cocktail of orange squash, baked beans and toothpaste made him so violently sick that he set light to the carpet. Dirk didn't work for dragons. Never had. Never would. Dragons were too much trouble. They asked too many questions, the answers to which could result in Dirk being arrested and hauled in front of the Council. He had got away with that once, he didn't fancy giving it another go.

In spite of all this, he said in a quiet, already regretful voice, "Yes."

"Thank you. Thank you, Mr Dirk!" exclaimed Alba, hugging him. "I know you'll be able to find Delfina! When do we start?" she asked.

"No time like the present." Dirk scribbled a note for Mrs K, which he left on his desk, and opened the window. "You said you were supposed to be meeting your sister in Spain."

"Yes."

"Then I guess we're off to Europe," replied Dirk.

For several hours Dirk and Alba headed south, above the clouds, occasionally ducking or swerving to avoid airplanes. They flew over the white cliffs of Dover, the English Channel and mainland Europe. Alba spoke incessantly but, to Dirk's relief, the rushing wind carried her words away unheard. Dirk thought about Holly. He had promised to call her back. He felt bad. She had sounded like she needed his help. He resolved to call her as soon as he got the chance.

He hadn't flown so far in years and soon his wings grew tired. Instead of flapping them he tried catching rising air currents, which felt warm against his soft green underbelly.

Eventually, with the sun rising and the sky growing lighter, Alba announced, "She lives down here."

Dirk flew down into the thinner part of the cloud. Below him was a rugged mountainous landscape where a cable-car ride ferried tourists up the rock face to take photos of the spectacular view. Luckily, being so early in the morning there were no tourists to snap pictures of the two dragons swooping down from the sky.

Dirk and Alba landed on a mountainside by a stream. Dirk breathed in the thin early morning air. It was fresh and cool. He surveyed the limestone valley. Living in London it was easy to forget that the world wasn't entirely crawling with human beings. Humans crammed themselves into the smallest of spaces, huddled together like scared animals, leaving vast areas like this uninhabited.

Alba pointed at a cave, halfway up a rock face, impossible to reach by foot. "That is where we meet every year."

She spread her wings and flew to the cave, followed closely by Dirk.

The cave was larger than it had appeared from the valley. It was damp and shadowy too. Dirk opened his mouth and breathed fire. His flame caught a pile of branches in the corner, setting them alight and filling the cave with flickering orange light.

"You see, Mr Dirk, she is not here," said Alba. "She has gone."

"What's this?" Dirk noticed a line of grey powder on the cave floor.

"I do not know," said Alba.

He licked his finger and dabbed it, inspecting it closely. "It's ash," he announced.

There was a line of ash around the cave. Dirk followed it.

"What does it mean?"

The trail led him back to where he had started, as

40

though the outline of ash formed an uneven circle. Then it hit him. He stood up on his hind legs and pushed Alba back.

"It can't be," he muttered.

"Cannot it be what?" said Alba.

The ash had been smudged by their footprints but the shape was still clear. The head. The wings. The tail. It was the outline of a dragon.

"But no one has seen this in hundreds of years," said Dirk.

"Seen what this?" asked Alba. "What is it all meaning?"

"A Sky Dragon has materialized here," said Dirk.

6

It was the first Saturday of the summer holiday and, after weeks of gazing out of stuffy classrooms at glorious sunny days, the sky was grey with the promise of rain. As Holly got off the bus, large drops began to fall.

She arrived at Dirk's office and rang the doorbell.

"Who is it?" called Mrs Klingerflim from behind the door.

"It's me, Holly."

There was a pause as Mrs Klingerflim fiddled with the countless locks. Eventually, the door opened and her owl-like face appeared. She smiled. "Hello, dear. Nice weather for ducks."

Holly stepped inside.

"Mind you, just because ducks like sitting on water, it doesn't mean they like it falling on their heads." She laughed. "I like sitting on comfy chairs but I wouldn't want to get caught in a sofa storm."

"Your umbrella would break," Holly added. "Is Dirk in?"

"I don't know – do you want to go and have a look? He was making a terrible racket last night. That awful man next door was complaining."

Holly took the stairs two at a time and knocked on Dirk's office door. There was no reply, so she entered his office. It was a tip. Dirk didn't have the highest cleaning standards at the best of times but this was more than the usual mess. She noticed the smashed television screen.

Mrs Klingerflim followed her in. "Oh dear," she said.

The rain was coming down so hard outside that it was splashing through the open window, dampening the carpet. Holly closed it. The traffic noises cut out, making the room seem suddenly quiet.

"I wonder where he's gone." Holly tidied up the bits of paper from the floor and shifted them into a pile in the corner. She picked up what looked like a black paperweight, then noticed the book on his desk. It was red with a white zigzagged line across the front. She opened it up and read the title.

Dragonlore
A Scientific Study of Dragons
by Ivor Klingerflim

Dirk had told her about it but he hadn't let her look at it, worried that she knew too much as it was.

Holly flicked through the pages. They were illustrated with line drawings. She turned to the chapter on Tree Dragons and shuddered at the memory of the ones she had met on her last case with Dirk.

"How long did it take Ivor to write?" she asked.

"His whole life." Mrs Klingerflim took the book from Holly and looked at it fondly. "Dragon-spotting requires a great deal of patience. Some people think fishing is boring but it's got nothing on dragon-spotting. Ivor and I would spend every spare moment camping out in some remote spot.

Sometimes we would come home after a month having seen nothing. But when you did see one, even just a glimpse, it made it all worthwhile. When you've seen the Desert Dragons of California at dusk … well." Mrs Klingerflim stopped to wipe a tear from her eye. She shut the book.

"Mrs Klingerflim, do you remember when I first came here, I said I was Dirk's niece?"

"Oh, yes. What a dreadful fib," said the old lady.

"But if you knew Dirk was a dragon, then you knew I was lying. Why did you let me in?"

"Ah, well. Dragons aren't the most sociable creatures, are they? They don't need friends and family like we do. But do you know, since Mr Dilly has been living among us I think he's picked up some of our habits. In a funny way, he's become a bit more human. And when you arrived after so cleverly tracking him down, I decided maybe you would make a good friend for him. Oh, look, a note." Mrs Klingerflim picked up a piece of paper on the desk. She held it right in front of her nose to read it. "It's no good," she said. "The writing's too small for my old eyes. What does it say?"

Holly took the note and read it out loud.

Mrs K,
Away on a case for a few days. Will pay
rent on return,
Dirk
P.S. Sorry about mess

"Ah, mystery solved."

There was an awkward pause while Holly tried not
to feel disappointed that he hadn't mentioned her in
the note.

The silence was broken by the doorbell.

"I wonder who that could be," said Mrs K, heading
down the stairs.

Holly put the note back on the desk, pushed the
window open and looked down. There were two men
standing on the doorstep: a tall one with a strand of
wet hair combed over his head and a shorter one,
whose curly red hair was made even curlier by the
rainfall. The tall man took a step back and Holly saw
his face.

She ducked back inside and shouted, "No, Mrs

Klingerflim! Don't answer it!" She ran to the landing but it was too late. Mrs Klingerflim was already opening the door and saying, "What can I do for you two gentlemen?"

"Ah, yes, please allow me to introduce myself. My name is Arthur Holt and this stocky gentleman is my friend and colleague, Mr Reginald Norman. We are two small-scale philanthropists, looking for ways to help the situation of the neighbourhood's elderly and infirm, vis-a-vis a non-profit-making all-encompassing service provider."

"We're odd-job men," added the other. "Except we don't charge."

7

The last time Holly had encountered Arthur and Reg, the two crooks were working for the mysterious Vainclaw Grandin, unaware that their boss was in fact a dragon who wanted to conquer and enslave their entire species.

"Well, my guttering needs looking at. Did you say you don't charge?" asked Mrs Klingerflim.

Holly tugged her sleeve. "You can't trust them," she said in her ear.

"What a charming little girl," said Arthur, smiling at her. "Is this your granddaughter?"

"No one does odd jobs for free," said Holly. "It doesn't make sense."

"That's what I thought," agreed Reg, nodding. "But

it's something to do with feet utensils."

"What my companion is trying to say is that Reginald and I are foot soldiers of utilitarianism," said Arthur.

"That's it," said Reg.

"It's a simple philosophy summed up in the sentiment *the greatest happiness for the greatest number of people*. My companion and I are trying to give something back to society."

"Not that we've taken nothing," said Reg quickly.

Arthur shook his head solemnly. "Oh, Reginald, let us not forget that we have occasionally stumbled on to the wrong side of the law. But now we are reborn, reformed and at your service."

"Are you selling something?" said Mrs Klingerflim.

Arthur laughed. "We are but two men standing in front of one elderly lady asking to do her guttering."

"We don't want anything from you," said Holly.

"Fair enough," said Arthur, backing away. "We understand. Have a good day, the both of you."

"And be happy," added Reg.

Mrs Klingerflim closed the door. "What a funny pair," she said.

"I need to go," stated Holly urgently.

"You've only just got here."

"Sorry, I've just remembered I need to be somewhere." She thought it best not to tell Mrs Klingerflim that she was actually off to follow the two crooks.

"Why don't you hang on to this?" said Mrs K, handing her the red book with the white zigzag across the front. "I think you'll find it quite interesting. Don't lose it, mind. It's my only copy."

"Thanks, I'll look after it." Holly slipped the book into her bag and left.

The rain had eased off. Arthur and Reg were on the opposite side of the road, knocking on another door. An elderly man answered. Holly couldn't hear what they were saying but it looked like they were giving him the same routine. The old man must have bought it because he invited them in. Holly checked for traffic, then crossed the road. Along the side of the house was a path where the residents kept their wheelie bins. The first gate on the right led to the old man's back garden. Holly headed down the path. She heard the back door open and Arthur's voice say,

"Yes, we are foot soldiers of utilitarianism."

She peeked through a gap in the wooden fence and saw the crooks walk into the garden and begin raking and tidying up leaves, while casually chatting to the old man.

"Why did you say you were doing this?" asked the man.

"We were once on the wrong side of the law, weren't we, Reg?" said Arthur.

"That's right. Rotten as a pair of bad bananas," said Reg.

"And then we had an awakening."

"It was like a miracle, weren't it, Arthur?"

"A miracle, indeed. I remember standing outside a train station somewhere – Stonegarth, I think it was called – when I felt a sharp slap on my cheek."

"I had the same thing," added Reg.

"It was as though we awoke from a strange dream," continued Arthur, "with the clear knowledge that from then on our mission was to make the world a better place."

"It brings a tear to my eye to think about it," said Reg. "And not just because of how hard the slap was."

Holly realized what had happened. The last time she had seen Arthur and Reg they had still been under the powerful hypnotic spell of Dirk's Dragonsong. She remembered how Dirk had leaned forwards and said something she couldn't hear. She realized he must have told them to give up crime and dedicate their lives to making the world a better place.

"Where do we put the bag?" asked Reg, tying it up and throwing it over his shoulder.

"Outside the gate, please," replied the old man.

The ill-fitting gate rattled. Holly quickly pressed herself against the fence and imagined what it was like to be this varnished wooden fence. As the gate opened she turned the same colour as the dark wood, vanishing from sight. Reg dropped the bag next to her. Just then, a phone started to ring.

"I think that's coming from you," said the old man.

"You seem to be correct," said Arthur. "I'd forgotten I even had a phone."

"Maybe you shouldn't answer it. It might be one of our old mates, asking us to do some dodgy job," said Reg.

"If it is indeed a member of the criminal community,

a scallywag, a ne'er-do-well, a rogue, I shall inform them of our new path, the long and winding road to happiness."

"Yeah, good idea," sad Reg, pulling the gate shut behind him. All three men went back into the house.

Holly moved and her natural colour returned.

"You have got to teach me how to do that," said an astonished voice.

She froze, then looked behind her to see a boy with blue eyes and dirty blond hair, balanced on top of a fence, staring at her in disbelief. Archie Snellgrove. For the last few weeks at school he had been her tormentor. Now, it appeared, he had just seen her using dragon powers. This was bad news indeed.

"Where are we to going now? Are you believing a Sky Dragon has taken Delfina? Why would they be doing that? Have you ever seen one? I have never seen one. Not materialized, at least."

Alba Longs was proving to be the most irritating dragon Dirk had ever met. It wasn't just the incessant chatter, either – she had a very annoying habit of poking Dirk with her claw every time she said something.

The dark chamber of rock shifted around them as they plummeted down. Dirk had asked the rock in Dragonspeak to take them down to the massive network of underground tunnels, where thousands of dragons dwelled, far out of the reach of humans.

They were heading for the lithosphere tunnel, the outermost arm of the matrix.

"We're going to see Karny," said Dirk.

"Captain Karnataka?" replied Alba. "How can he be helping us? He was the one who sent me to you."

"Karny always knows what's going on in the dragon world and now that he's got thousands of Drakes answering to him he'll be even better informed. If the Skies are on the move he'll know about it."

"I am not sure this is the best plan," said Alba. "I do not like those Drakes. Horrible creatures."

Dirk nodded in agreement. Drab-nosed Drakes were fireless, wingless dragons with floppy noses, big bellies and small brains.

The rock beneath Dirk and Alba's claws pulled away and they dropped into a large tunnel lit with the dim orange glow of earthlight.

Dirk stood up and dusted himself down. "Now, if memory serves me correctly, Dragnet HQ is this way," he said.

"I do not think the captain will be able to help us."

"Karny and I go back a long way," said Dirk, walking down the tunnel. "Besides, it's his fault I'm involved in this. I've still got a case on the go back in London. The sooner I can solve this one, the better."

"But you care why my sister has been vanished?"

"It's just work." Dirk shrugged. "The first thing you learn as a detective is to never let it get personal."

Behind him, Alba let out a long wailing noise. "Ahhh!" she cried.

"Don't be so melodramatic," said Dirk, refusing to turn around.

"Get off me!" squealed Alba.

Dirk spun around to see Alba with a black metal cuff attached to her neck. He felt a sharp pain as an identical cuff snapped round his own neck.

"You is under arrest, boy," said the dust-grey Drake with the chain attached to his short, stumpy tail.

Dirk reared up on to his hind legs and roared fire, but the flames bounced off the Drake's armour-like skin. The Dragnet officer swung his tail down, dragging Dirk to the ground.

"Good work, Junior," said the Drake holding Alba. "That's it, show this traitor who's boss."

With their long, floppy noses and inflated bellies, Drakes looked almost comical, but Dirk knew well that once a Dragnet officer had a dragon cuffed, there was no way out. Iron or steel Dirk could have bitten through, but Dragnet chains were made from black metal, forged in the liquid fires of the Outer Core. It was ten times stronger than any metal known to humans.

"You hold on tight now, Junior," said the larger of the two Drakes.

"Sure thing, Pappy," said the smaller one, swinging his tail so that Dirk felt another painful jolt around his neck.

"You are hurt my skin," complained Alba.

"On what grounds are you arresting us, Drake?" Dirk addressed the older Drake.

"You speak to Pappy with respect." The younger Drake yanked Dirk's chain again.

"Well done, Junior," said Pappy. "You'll make a fine Dragnet officer, just like your old pappy and my pappy before me. And his pappy, your great-grand pappy. And his pappy, your great-great-grand—"

"On what grounds?" interrupted Dirk, his head throbbing.

"Tell him, Junior," said Pappy.

"We is arresting you on grounds that we is currently in a state of emergency as declared by our glorious captain, Karnataka the Fearless."

"Karnataka the Fearless?" laughed Dirk. He had heard Karny described as a lot of things but never fearless. "Why has Karny declared a state of emergency?"

"The Kinghorns are on the rise," said Junior. "There's talk that they're gathering an army, preparing for the big attack. Captain Karnataka has told us to arrest any dragon acting suspiciously and you two is definitely suspicious."

"But we are looking for my sister," said Alba.

"Sounds mighty suspicious to me," said Pappy. "What do you think, Junior?"

"Mighty suspicious, Pappy."

"We are not doing anything the wrong," pleaded Alba.

"The captain has declared a state of emergency," said Pappy, "and you two is sure-fire criminal types."

"No, this is Mr Dirk Dilly," said Alba. "He is a famous detective. I am Alba Longs. Mr Dirk is helping me to find my sister."

"Keep quiet, Alba," snarled Dirk.

"Famous detective, eh?" said Pappy. "Well, I'm a bit of a detective myself and I detect the blood of a couple of Kinghorns."

Dirk sighed. He had learned from previous experience that for all their self-importance, Dragnet officers were almost always looking for what they could get out of a situation. He was yet to meet one who couldn't be bribed.

"OK," he said. "What will it take to persuade you to let us go?"

Junior pulled hard on the chain, bringing Dirk's face close. "You can't bribe Pappy," he said. "My pappy is the most honestest officer in the Dragnet. He ain't never taken a back-hander. Ain't that right, Pappy?"

"Er … sure thing, son," said Pappy, although Dirk could see from the look on his face that if his son hadn't been there it would have been a different story.

"Rats," muttered Dirk. "Of all the Drakes in the world we had to meet these two prize specimens."

"What was that, Mountain Dragon?" said Pappy.

"I said, we'll come quietly."

"You see, Junior. Now he's showing some respect.

All these dragons understand is a firm cuff."

The two Drakes set off down the tunnel, pulling Alba and Dirk behind them.

"How can we find Delfina now?" said Alba.

"Never mind her," replied Dirk. "How are we going to get out of this?"

"Surely they will let us go when they realize we are innocent," she said.

"You two Kinghorns keep quiet!" yelled Junior.

"You tell them no good traitors, Junior," said Pappy.

"Oh yes," said Dirk under his breath. "They seem like a very open-minded pair."

Holly had been so intent on spying on the crooks that she hadn't checked whether anyone else was watching. She could have kicked herself for being so careless but that wouldn't have got her anywhere. Instead, she let her face relax into a smile and laughed.

"So this is how you spend your holidays, is it? Following people?"

"I was in the area when I saw you cross the road then … er, well, you vanished. How did you do that?" Archie jumped down from the fence into the alleyway.

"Do what?" replied Holly, a picture of wide-eyed innocence.

"Turn invisible," said Archie. "Don't deny it. I saw it with my own eyes."

"Good luck getting anyone else to believe that," she retorted.

"Why would I tell anyone else?" Archie grinned, reached into his pocket and pulled out a jelly baby. He brushed off the pocket fluff and threw it into his mouth. "Can you show me how to do it?"

"No," said Holly. "We're not friends. All you've done is tease me since I came to the school."

"I tease everyone."

"You said I was posh."

"I've seen your house," countered Archie.

"And then you went on about my stepmum losing her stupid job as an MP. Like I even care about politics."

Archie smiled. "I'm sorry about all that. I was just teasing. And maybe I was following you, but only because I thought you were interesting. And you really are. Interesting, I mean. So can you show me how to turn invisible now?"

"No, we're not friends."

"Yes but we could be," said Archie.

"I'm not sure I want to be," said Holly.

"Allies then," said Archie.

"Allies against who?"

"Against the world," said Archie, gesticulating wildly. "What do you say? I mean, you don't exactly seem to have a lot of friends and none of mine are as interesting as you."

Archie held out a hand. His nails were dirty, his T-shirt was stained, but there was something about the way his smile showed in his eyes at that moment that made Holly want to trust him.

Dirk had once told her that the art of telling a good lie was to tell as much of the truth as possible and change only one or two key details.

"It isn't exactly turning invisible," she replied. "It's called blending and it's easy, you just have to stay very still and think like whatever it is you're trying to blend with."

The only thing she failed to mention was the minor detail that first you needed to swallow Mountain Dragon blood.

Pappy locked the cell door, securing Alba and Dirk inside.

"I want to be getting out!" cried Alba through the small barred window in the door.

"Now, Junior," said Pappy. "You stay here and guard the convicts while I go and alert the Petty Patrol Officer."

"What will he do, Pappy?"

"He'll inform the Chief Area Patrol Officer, who will tell the local magistrate, who will bring up the matter with the Dragnet Regional Manager at the next bi-millennial meeting. The Regional Manager reports directly to Captain Karnataka."

"Couldn't you just tell Captain Karnataka yourself?" interjected Dirk. "I'm an old friend of his."

Pappy turned to look at him. "This is Dragnet procedure. Tell them why we have procedure, Junior."

"Because procedure is all that stands between Dragnet order and dragon chaos," replied his son.

"Very good. Now, I won't be too long. You keep this door shut tight."

"Yes, Pappy."

"Remember, dragons can be tricksy. No matter

what they say to you, do not open this door."

"Yes, Pappy."

"That's my boy."

Pappy waddled away down the corridor.

"What are we to do now?" asked Alba.

"There's not much we *can* do," replied Dirk. "Black metal was used to build these cells. It runs through the rock. The only way out is through that locked door. And the thing about that locked door is that it's locked."

"But you said Captain Karnataka was your friend. He will let us out."

"You heard them. It could be months before news gets to Karny."

"Years," said a low voice, which made them both jump. It came from the back of the cell. "I've been here for six hundred and twenty-two years, four months and three days and my case hasn't even got as far as the magistrate yet."

Dirk could just about make out two eyes set in a head as black as coal. "Who are you?" he demanded.

"I'll exchange my name for yours," said the dragon, standing to reveal a yellow underbelly.

"The name's Dirk Dilly. This is Alba Longs. And if I'm not mistaken, you're a yellow-bellied, coal-black Cave Dweller," said Dirk.

The dragon nodded. "They call me Fairfax Nordstrum," he said. "Well, they used to call me that when anyone called me anything." He spoke slowly, as though carefully considering every word before speaking it. "I've counted the days of my imprisonment on the wall."

Dirk saw that the cell wall was covered in small lines scratched into the rock.

"What did they put you in for?" he asked.

"That's the funny thing, I can't actually remember. When my trial comes up I won't know whether to plead guilty or innocent." He smiled wryly. "And what brings you to my little home?"

"Mr Dilly is a detective," said Alba. "He is helping me to finding my sister. But in the cave where I was to be meeting my sister, Mr Dilly found an outline of ash and this means that a Sky Dragon materialized there and I always thought Sky Dragons were just stories but then we met two Drakes and they threw us in this cell and now we are being on the wrong side of a locked door and we still haven't found my sis—"

"You talk too much," Dirk growled at Alba.

"I can help you find your sister," said Fairfax.

"You can?" asked Alba. "How? Do you know her? Have you seen her?"

"No, but I know where Sky Dragons go after materializing."

"Where?" asked Dirk.

"I'll tell you if you help me," he replied.

"Help you do what?"

"Get out," spoke Fairfax. "Get me out of this cell and I will tell you where you can find this Sky Dragon you seek."

Junior was feeling mightily pleased with himself. He had assisted his pappy in capturing two traitors and now he had the very important job of guarding the cell until Pappy got back.

"But if we cannot be getting out, we will not be able to attend the meeting of secrets," said one of the prisoners.

Junior's ears pricked up. It was the Sea Dragon, Alba Longs.

"You mean the secret meeting," replied the Mountain Dragon called Dirk Dilly. "When all the Kinghorns in the world will be gathering in one place?"

"That is what I am meaning, yes, the secret

Kinghorn meeting when all the Kinghorns in the world will be gathering in one place."

"Will you keep your voice down about the secret Kinghorn meeting?" hushed Dirk.

"What does it matter? We are stuck in this cell."

"Someone might overhear." The Mountain Dragon had lowered his voice but Junior put his ear to the door so he could still hear. "If that Dragnet Officer out there overheard – and if he was smart – he would cook up a devious plan."

What sort of plan? thought Junior.

"What sort of plan?" asked the Sea Dragon.

"He could unlock the door, wait for us to escape, then follow us to the secret location."

Junior listened intently.

"Why would he do that?"

"Because then he could bring more officers and arrest every single Kinghorn in one go," said Dirk.

"Wow, that would be bad for us but good for him. They would probably be giving him a medal," replied Alba.

"They'd cover him in medals. So you'd better keep your voice down about the *you know what*."

"You mean, the secret meeting of all the Kinghorns?"

"Exactly."

Junior's mind was working overtime. This was big. Really big. Pappy had told him to keep the door locked no matter what the traitors said to him, but they hadn't said anything *to* him. What they had said, he had overheard and how could they trick him if they didn't know he was listening?

Junior resolved to follow his instincts. He unlocked the door and crept back into the shadows.

It didn't take long for the door to open and the Mountain Dragon's head to appear.

"The door's open," he said. "Come on, the coast is clear."

Junior held his paw to his mouth to stop himself from chuckling at their foolishness.

The door opened wider and the two other dragons stepped out.

"Does this mean we can go to the secret meeting after all?" asked the Sea Dragon.

"Be quiet about the secret meeting," scolded the Mountain Dragon. "You never know who might be listening. Come on. Let's go."

Junior removed the chain and cuff from his tail so that he could follow them without clinking. However, the feeling of immense pride that was growing in his large belly suddenly vanished when something whacked him on the head. He stumbled forwards and landed face first, pinned to the ground by an unseen assailant.

The two dragons turned around.

"I order you to release me. I am an officer of the Dragnet," he protested.

Junior couldn't see who was restraining him, but he could feel the weight on his back and the claws digging into his skin.

"This is for all those years in that cell," whispered Fairfax Nordstrum.

"Don't hurt him," said Dirk. "Just take him back to the cell."

Junior was hauled backwards, struggling and thrashing but outnumbered and outwitted. The Mountain Dragon attached the cuff around his neck before throwing him into the cell and locking the door.

"You're being awful silly. Locking a Dragnet officer

in a cell is against the law, you no good traitors," Junior said through the grate in the door.

"I'll leave you the key then," replied Dirk, dropping it within sight but out of reach. "And don't call me silly," he snarled.

Junior had been tricked. "Don't leave me here!" he begged.

"Your imprisonment will be a blink of an eye compared to mine," said the Cave Dweller bitterly.

Junior groaned. "But you can't leave me like this," he said.

"Your pappy will be back soon enough," said Dirk.

"That's what I'm worried about," replied Junior.

11

Upstairs on the bus home, Archie spent the whole journey trying unsuccessfully to blend with the grubby chequered seat.

"You're not sitting still enough," said Holly, smiling to herself.

"The bus is too bumpy," complained Archie.

"Try it later, when you're at home."

The thought of Archie spending hours trying to think like a sofa, without moving a muscle, was sweet revenge for his behaviour in school.

Holly pressed the bell and stood up. "This is my stop."

"Can I come with you?" pleaded Archie, following her downstairs and off the bus.

"No, you can't." Holly still had Mrs Klingerflim's book in her bag and she wanted to get home and read it. "You can come and call for me tomorrow if you want," she suggested, striding off.

"Can't I come round now?" asked Archie, catching up with her.

"Why?"

"I want to see how the other half live," replied Archie, winking.

"I'm not the other half," insisted Holly.

But Archie didn't give up easily. He was still there when Holly reached her door, so she relented. "You can come in but only for a minute."

As they approached her front door, she felt nervous. Her whole life, she had never brought a friend home. If 'friend' was even the right word for Archie. Holly intended to sneak in but, as she pulled out her key, the front door swung open to reveal her stepmum on her way out.

Mrs Bigsby looked down. "Oh, Holly. I didn't know you'd gone out."

"Where are you going?" Holly noticed that her stepmum was looking suspiciously smart.

74

"That's none of your business," she replied.

"You've taken the job, haven't you?"

Holly's dad stepped out of the living room. "Holly," he said. "Oh, you've got a friend."

"Hello," said Archie, apparently relishing the awkwardness of the moment. "I've never met a real-life politician before."

"Then you still haven't. I am no longer a member of parliament," said Mrs Bigsby haughtily. "Although I would not rule out the possibility of serving my country in the future, at present I am exploring other avenues."

"Such as working for a man who hurts animals," said Holly angrily.

"Now, Holly…" began her father.

"One cannot change the world if one is not engaged with it," said Mrs Bigsby.

"And paid a lot for it," added Holly.

"We need the money," snapped Mrs Bigsby. "Now, please get out of my way, both of you. I have a car waiting outside."

Reluctantly, Holly stepped aside, allowing her stepmum to leave. Holly's dad turned to Archie.

"So are you at school with Holly? I'm glad to see she's made a friend."

"Oh, we're really good friends," said Archie. "We're totally transparent with each other."

Holly's dad smiled at this, apparently not picking up on what an odd thing this was to say. He left them to it.

"So what are we going to do now?" asked Archie.

"We're going back out," replied Holly.

"Out? We've only just got in."

"We need to follow my stepmum. We can't just sit back and let her take a job with a man who hurts animals," said Holly.

Archie's grin widened. "Oh, I knew becoming your friend was a good idea."

Once the three dragons reached a safe distance from the cell, Dirk stopped and turned to Fairfax Nordstrum. "I kept my side of the bargain. Now it's your turn. Where will I find this Sky Dragon?"

They were standing in the dim orange glow of the lithosphere tunnel.

"First things first," purred Fairfax, fixing his eyes

on Dirk. "I've been shut up in that cell a long time. I'd like to know what's changed since I've been away."

"We had a deal," said Dirk. "I need to find this Sea Dragon's sister so I can get back to work."

"Your detective work, yes," said the Cave Dweller. "That does sound fascinating. What sorts of things do you..." He paused to emphasize the word, "*detect?*"

"It's none of your business," Dirk growled, smoke billowing threateningly from both nostrils.

"Calm down," replied Fairfax casually. "I have no intention of going back on our bargain. I just want to know what's been going on during the last six hundred years."

"Nothing much has changed. Humans still roam the earth, dragons still hide," said Dirk.

"And are the Kinghorns really on the rise again as those Drakes said?"

"I am hearing they are planning to start a war," said Alba.

"And who is leading them in this war?"

Alba lowered her voice. "A Mountain Dragon

called Vainclaw Grandin. They call him the first up-airer."

"Enough," said Dirk, whose only encounter with the Kinghorn leader had almost cut short his own life. "If you don't tell us where to find the Sky Dragon, I'll blacken that yellow belly of yours."

"No need for threats. I said I would tell you and I will," said Fairfax. "As you know, all dragons get energy from the earthlight that emanates from the Inner Core."

Dirk nodded. It was the earthlight that lit these tunnels far beneath the surface of the earth. It was as important to dragons as sunlight was to humans.

"Sky Dragons need it as much as we do," continued Fairfax. "But when they have spent a long time as gas, floating high, far from the source of their power, they are considerably weakened. After materializing they are exhausted and faint. A small dose of sugar will revive them temporarily but what they really need is to recharge with earthlight energy."

"So they come underground?" asked Dirk.

"Not just underground. When they materialize they need to build up their strength so they go to the banks of the Outer Core where they bathe in the liquid fire. It's painful but effective. A Sky Dragon at full strength is a powerful dragon indeed."

"How do you know all this?" asked Dirk.

Fairfax's mouth curled into a smile. "I have been around a long time. I've seen a lot of things. I remember a time when Sky Dragons roamed free, rather than hiding among the clouds. I've never heard of one kidnapping a Sea Dragon, though."

Dirk considered whether he had been rash in freeing Fairfax Nordstrum. There was something distinctly sinister about the Cave Dweller.

"Where will you go now, Nordstrum?" he asked.

"I'll probably just go and find some quiet corner of the world to curl up in. I've been living on dirt for the last six hundred years. My needs aren't great. I just want somewhere quiet with fresh vegetation. The Andes, perhaps, or a little island somewhere."

"Good luck with that," said Dirk.

Then, speaking in the ancient language of Dragonspeak, Dirk asked the rock beneath his feet to take Alba and him down to the banks of the Outer Core. The rock, being rock, obliged unquestioningly and lowered the two dragons.

"And good luck with your detecting," said Fairfax as they vanished.

12

Archie was both impressed and unnerved by how easily Holly was able to follow her stepmum using an app on her phone.

"My dad gave me this old phone of his, then downloaded all this tracking software to keep tabs on me," she explained. "But he didn't really understand it so he asked me to help set it up. I've made it so I can trace their phones instead."

The dot representing Mrs Bigsby's phone stopped in a part of London called Kennington. Holly pressed the button marked 'Directions' and found the quickest route. As they stood waiting at the bus stop, Archie asked, "So you do this sort of thing a lot, do you? Follow family members?"

"Following people is pretty standard detective work," replied Holly casually.

"And you're a detective?"

"Sort of. My uncle is. I help him out sometimes."

"Your uncle is a detective?"

"Yes. His name is Dirk Dilly."

"That sounds made up." Archie chuckled.

"It isn't," Holly spoke firmly, then thought about it for a moment. "At least I don't think he made it up."

"You don't think your uncle made up his own name?"

"He's quite secretive." Holly wondered if she had said too much.

"What's his agency called?"

"It's not important. Look, the bus is coming now."

Archie continued to ask about Dirk for the whole bus journey, but Holly refused to tell him. After twenty minutes or so, they got off the bus and walked the rest of the way, through a park to a busy road lined with coffee shops, hairdressers and estate agents. In between these, set back from the road, behind a set of tall silver gates was a flat-roofed two-storey building, that would have been unremarkable in appearance were it not for the group of protesters outside, waving placards with slogans that read:

ANIMALS HAVE RIGHTS TOO!

GLOBAL SANDS:
BLOOD ON YOUR HANDS!

EXPERIMENT ON BUCHANAN INSTEAD!

A couple of sturdy-looking policemen stood between the crowd and the gates.

"This must be the lab I read about," said Holly.

One of the protestors had a loudhailer and was making a speech.

"Brant Buchanan sits up there in his ivory tower. Well, I've got news for you, Mr Buchanan. Ivory is illegal in this country and when we knock down your tower you'll come tumbling down to earth. And that's both a metaphor and true."

"There must be a side door," said Holly.

"How do you know that?" Archie asked.

"Because my stepmother is in there and there is

no way she would be caught going through an angry mob like this."

She showed Archie the little dot on the phone indicating Mrs Bigsby's location inside the building.

"There must be another way in. Follow me."

They circled the building until they found a narrow alleyway with a locked door on the same side as the building. Archie moved to take a closer look but Holly stopped him.

"There's a camera," she said, pointing. "They check who you are before opening it, but I'd bet that if some scruffy-looking kid was to cause a fuss outside, a security guard would come down and shoo him away."

"You want me to help you break into a building in order to follow your stepmum because you don't want her working for a billionaire who experiments on animals?" said Archie.

"Yes," said Holly, deciding not to mention the AOG project or the secret weapon that Brant was trying to get his hands on.

"Fine," said Archie. "So what do you want me to do?"

"What I just said. Cause a distraction."

"Oh yes. Brilliant."

Archie was loving every minute of his day with Holly. When he first decided to follow her that morning, he had thought it might prove a fun diversion, but it was exceeding all his expectations. Detectives, invisible girls, sinister billionaires and cunning plans. He had never experienced anything like Holly's world before but he liked it and suspected there were more surprises to come.

He watched as the colour drained from the tips of Holly's fingers, her face and then the rest of her body. Even her clothes and shoes turned the colour of the wall behind her, until all that was left were her brown eyes staring back at him.

"So cool," he muttered under his breath.

"Get on with it." Holly's mouth briefly appeared as she spoke.

Archie approached the door, pressed the buttons on the buzzer and pulled silly faces at the screen. Eventually the door opened and a burly, uniformed security guard with a thick black moustache appeared.

"Go away," he said.

"Can't I come in?" asked Archie.

"Noh a chance," replied the security guard in a thick Scottish accent.

"But I live here," he protested.

"Right, and I'm the Duchess of Kent."

"Your majesty," said Archie, bowing.

The security guard stepped forwards threateningly. Archie saw Holly reappear and slip behind the man, through the door.

"I'll set the dogs on you if you don't clear off," said the large man.

"Sorry for wasting your time," said Archie, turning around and walking away with a smile on his face.

13

"I did not trust that Cave-Dweller. He had darkness in his eyes. He had been locked away a long time. Imagine having not anyone to talk to for all that time … just you and your own thinkings. Can you imagine it? No one but you."

Dirk imagined it. It sounded nice. There was something about travelling by rock that made Alba talk incessantly.

"But there is one thing I am not understanding," she continued. "If a Sky Dragon is so weak when it materializes, how could one be kidnapping my sister? Delfina is a strong dragon."

"We don't know much about them," replied Dirk. "I've never seen one. Not in the flesh, at least.

What bothers me is why a Sky Dragon would want to kidnap a Sea Dragon at all."

"I have heard that Sky Dragons think they are above us."

"Funny that," said Dirk.

Alba didn't get the joke. "I heard they can make firewalls, although I do not know what a firewall is. A wall of fire, I suppose…"

While Alba wittered on, Dirk's mind wandered. He found himself thinking about Holly. He had become so wrapped up in this case that he had forgotten about her. He hoped she wasn't getting herself into too much trouble. He would make it up to her when he got back and take her for a trip over London.

As they neared their destination the pocket of shifting rock that surrounded them grew brighter and hotter, making Alba jumpy.

"This does not seem right to me. The banks of the Outer Core are only for pregnant dragons," she said.

"And convicted criminals," said Dirk grimly, "but they don't stop at the banks."

Only a handful of dragons had ever been banished to the earth's Inner Core by the Dragon Council but of those who had, none had returned.

"What do you think it is like down there?" asked Alba.

Dirk thought about it. The blinding light and incessant heat would be unbearable. "I can't imagine," said Dirk. "And I don't plan on finding out."

"Do you think it is possible to be surviving down there?" asked Alba.

"It's probably better if you can't," replied Dirk.

Even this far down, the air was stifling and Dirk had to squint at Alba in the dazzling earthlight.

"Brace yourself. I think we're there," he said, feeling the rock pull away from under his feet.

They tumbled on to a stony shoreline. Dirk felt disorientated. It was an odd sensation. He felt unsure which way up he was. An acute burning feeling in his belly made him cry "Yee-ouch!" and he jumped to his feet.

The scorching pebbles were painful on the tough skin of his feet but they were agony on his soft green underbelly.

At the edge of the shoreline was an ocean of liquid fire, bubbling, popping and spitting. It seemed to go on forever, steam rising up, obscuring the horizon.

"Welcome to the banks of the Outer Core, dudes."

The greeting came from a Firedrake, sitting on the edge of the shore. Firedrakes were relatives of the Drab-nosed Drakes and had the same large bellies and tough skin, but their noses were upturned and their backs were covered in tiny holes. This one wore what looked like a pair of crudely carved sunglasses and held a long black ladle. By his side were rows of black metal flasks. He dipped the ladle into the sizzling liquid, scooped some up and poured it into a flask. He then lifted it to his mouth, gulped it down greedily, licked his lips and burped, sending blasts of steam shooting from his mouth, nostrils and all the holes on his back.

"Wow, that tickles," said the Firedrake, leaning back and laughing.

"I think this one is peculiar inside the mind," said Alba, tapping the side of her head.

"Let's say hello," replied Dirk, approaching.

The Firedrake turned to look at them. "Hey, dragon dudes, what's happening?"

"The name's Dirk Dilly," he replied. "Why are you

drinking that stuff, Firedrake?"

"It's my job, dude… But I tell you what, after a while you develop a taste for it… The name's Shute." The Firedrake extended a paw.

Dirk shook it. "Shute?"

"Shute Hobcraft, Firedrake, at your service," he said, taking another sip of liquid fire, shooting out steam and bursting into hysterics.

"How can you drink something so hot?" said Alba.

"You wanna try some? I've got some vintage stuff here," he said, holding up a flask. "It really clears out your passages."

"We're looking for a dragon," said Dirk, already growing tired of the idiotic creature.

"There's one next to you," giggled Shute, pointing at Alba.

"We're looking for a *Sky* Dragon."

"A Sky Dragon. Whoa, dude. I haven't seen one of those for years."

"Come on, Alba." Dirk was getting annoyed. "Let's check further along the bank."

"There's no point," said Shute. "I can tell you, no Sky Dragon has been down this far in a long time."

Dirk turned to face him. "How can you be so sure?"

"I'll tell you if you have a swig," he replied, holding out the flask, sniggering.

"I'm losing my patience," said Dirk.

"Come on, I know you're going to like it," insisted Shute.

"All right, just one," said Dirk, taking the flask and looking warily at the bubbling liquid. He lifted it to his lips and took the tiniest of sips. The pain was immense. Dirk enjoyed a vegetable vindaloo as much as the next dragon, but this was seriously scorching. Dragons needed fairly hardy insides to breathe fire but they didn't have the same kind of internal insulation as Firedrakes.

"Yeaahhhhhouch!" Dirk screamed out in agony.

Shute found this hilarious and fell about laughing. "It's good, isn't it?"

"How can you be sure that no Sky Dragon has been this far down?" said Dirk, his tongue still burning.

"Because when a dragon plunges into the liquid fire of the Outer Core, the temperature drops. For Sky Dragons doubly so," said Shute. "My job is to test it. If it's one degree cooler I alert the authorities."

"Why?" asked Dirk.

"Because it probably means that a dragon has tried to escape the Inner Core. The bigger the dragon, the bigger the temperature drop. You should have tried it when Minertia went down. It was, like, cool, dude. She was one big dragon. The same would happen if a Sky Dragon took a dip."

"Minertia was convicted thirty years ago," said Dirk.

"Old Shute's been here for coming up on two hundred years now. Still, I don't mind. As I say I've got to like the stuff," said Shute, taking another ladleful, pouring it into a flask and taking a swig. After reappearing from the cloud of steam in a fit of giggles, he said, "All I know is that no Sky Dragon has been down here for a long time."

"Thanks for your help," said Dirk.

"No problem," said Shute. "Here, take one if you like." He held up a flask with a top on.

"No, thanks," said Dirk, his mouth still burning.

Alba grabbed the flask and said, "I will take it as a souvenir. Thank you."

"Keep up the good work," said Dirk, turning away.

"Hey, thanks, dragon," said Shute. "It's been a blast talking to you. Good luck finding that Sky Dragon."

"I told you he was peculiar in the brain," said Alba as they left.

"None of this makes sense," said Dirk. He was beginning to feel frustrated.

"If only we knew more about the Sky Dragons," said Alba.

Dirk looked at Alba. "Great rats of Grimsby!" he exclaimed. "That's it."

"What is what?" she replied.

Dirk couldn't believe he hadn't thought of it earlier. *Dragonlore*. Ivor Klingerflim had written an entire chapter on Sky Dragons. He felt behind his wing but it wasn't there. He must have left it in his office, which meant one thing.

He was going back to London.

14

Holly slipped behind the security man, through the doorway and pushed herself against the inside wall, turning white and vanishing from view. The security guard pulled the door shut again and walked down the corridor.

Once he was gone, Holly reappeared and made her way cautiously in the opposite direction. For a moment she doubted the wisdom of her actions. Why was she breaking into a high security lab? The answer came to her in the form of a purr. Something brushed against her leg. Holly looked down to see a tabby cat.

"Hello," she said.

The cat ignored her and continued walking down the corridor.

Holly followed it, passing a window that looked into a room full of cages with mice, cats and other animals inside. A door on the far side of the room opened and a young woman in a lab coat entered. She carried a plastic container with air holes in the top. Holly blended her head with the window, turning as transparent as the glass. The female lab-worker placed the container on the counter and opened one of the cages. A white mouse walked out of the cage into the container. The woman shut the cage door, picked up the container and left the room.

Holly continued down the corridor, ever prepared to stop, freeze and blend if necessary.

The cat passed a stairwell on the left, then stepped through a cat flap in a door on the right. Holly stopped outside the door and looked through a pane of glass into a small room. The cat sat in a basket in the corner. By its side were two bowls, one of milk, another of cat food. The cat must have been very well fed because it didn't seem at all interested in either bowl. Willow would have greedily emptied both bowls no matter how much she had already eaten.

Holly tried the door handle, half expecting it to

be locked but, to her surprise, the door opened. She entered the room, bent down and stroked the tabby. The cat made no response. It didn't purr or tilt its head so she could scratch it behind the ear, like Willow did. Nor did it flinch or move away. In fact it showed no sign of noticing, let alone enjoying the attention.

Holly examined the metallic collar around the cat's neck. She twisted it round and saw on the underside the letters G and S in a circle: the Global Sands logo.

Behind her she heard an electronic whirring, a noise she recognized immediately. The last time she had heard that sound she had been planning an escape from William Scrivener School. She spun around to find a security camera pointing at her. She ran to the door and desperately tried the handle. It was locked. She tried to find a blind spot, where she could vanish, but the camera followed her every move. She couldn't risk being seen blending. There was nowhere to hide. All she could do was sit and wait to be discovered.

"This is your fault," she said to the cat.

The animal remained perfectly still except for the gentle movement of its breathing.

When the door opened she looked up at the

security guard. She had only seen him from behind before, but now she instantly recognized the black bushy moustache as belonging to Hamish Fraser, the same guard she had encountered while trying to escape from William Scrivener's.

"It *is* you. I wasn't sure from the picture on the monitor," he said in his familiar Scottish accent. "What a small world it is. What brings you here, I wonder?"

Holly thought fast. "I came to find a toilet. I must have gone through the wrong door."

"Nice try," said Hamish, a grin spreading beneath his moustache. "You accidentally stumbled into a maximum-security building looking for the lavvy? You'll have to do better than that, lassie."

"Why aren't you at the school?" asked Holly.

"The school's shut for summer. I work here for a few months of the year. I'm on the late shift. I'm not so keen on being locked up with all these animals but, thanks to you, it's already proving more exciting than I'd expected."

"Where's Bruno?" asked Holly, remembering the poodle Hamish had tried to train to be more aggressive.

"Bruno? In this place?" said Hamish, gesticulating towards the cat. "He'd have a field day."

"What's wrong with this cat?" asked Holly, trying to stroke the unresponsive animal again.

"Don't worry about the moggy. Come on." Hamish began to frogmarch her out.

"Can't you just let me go for old time's sake?" she pleaded.

Hamish laughed a loud throaty laugh and said, "The last time I saw you I was trying to stop you breaking out. This time you've broken in. You're a right wee criminal in the making, aren't you?" He led Holly up the stairs she'd passed before. At the top he said, "In you go," and pushed the door open.

The room she walked into was a stark contrast to the rest of the building. Instead of white walls and a tiled floor, it had cream walls and a plush green carpet. Buchanan sat behind a desk made entirely from glass. At the other end of the room, Holly's stepmum sat on a purple sofa, staring at her, aghast and furious.

"The irrepressible Holly Bigsby," said Mr Buchanan, standing to greet her.

Holly avoided eye contact with Mrs Bigsby but

could feel her furious glare burning a hole in the back of her head.

"Your mother is angry with you but I am impressed," said Mr Buchanan.

"*Step*mother," said Holly.

The billionaire bowed his head, acknowledging his mistake. "When I designed this laboratory I knew that ill-informed animal activists and prying investigative journalists would try to get in. So there are no windows on the ground floor and these on the upper floor don't open. Both entrances, front and back, are under constant surveillance. The roof is made out of a synthetic material too strong to be cut by any conventional tool. No one has ever got further than the silver gates without my say so. Except you."

Holly said nothing.

"What really annoys them, you see," continued Mr Buchanan, "is that for all their protests and leaflets and slogans, they have absolutely no idea what we do here. For all they know we're making marmalade."

"You don't make marmalade," interjected Holly. "You experiment on animals."

"Everyone experiments on animals," said the billionaire. "When NASA sends an astronaut into space or when a country sends a soldier off to war. When a politician tries out a new policy or a teacher tries a new lesson plan. These are all animal experiments. Only the animals are humans. Why should our furry friends be excluded just because they can't talk, write or hold a gun?"

"I don't care how cleverly you say it, you're still hurting animals."

"You're too young to understand," said Mr Buchanan dismissively. "Now, I need to check that you haven't taken anything from my laboratory. Empty your pockets."

Holly did so, hoping he wouldn't notice the book-shaped bulge in her bag.

Too late. "What's that?" he asked.

"It's just a book." She shrugged.

"May I see it?"

"No."

"Holly," hissed Mrs Bigsby, finally breaking her silence. "You have trespassed on Mr Buchanan's property, you have insulted him. I can't begin to tell you how … how disappointed I am. Your father will be livid. Now, do as you are told."

Holly pulled out the book and handed it to Mr Buchanan across the desk. "It's just a silly book about mythical creatures, anyway," she muttered under her breath.

He took it but his gaze remained on her open palm.

"Your hand has healed remarkably quickly," he said.

"It wasn't that bad after all," replied Holly, whipping it away.

"Once again, I'm sorry for my husband's daughter, Brant," said Mrs Bigsby.

"Not at all, Angela. My driver, Weaver, will take you both home."

Buchanan pressed a button and spoke through the intercom. "Weaver, prepare the car."

"Can I have my book back?" said Holly, trying to sound casual, not wanting them to know how important it was.

"You'll get your book back when you've learned your lesson," replied Mrs Bigsby.

"I'll hang on to it if you like," offered Mr Buchanan.

"I've always had a soft spot for myths. Dragons were my favourite as a child."

He slipped it into the top drawer of his desk.

"Thank you," said Mrs Bigsby.

As the desk was made entirely of glass, Holly could still see the book easily enough but Buchanan locked the drawer and her stepmum led her out of the room. She felt bad. She had promised Mrs Klingerflim she would look after it but now there was no chance of getting it back.

16

Archie had been leaning against the wall outside the door, just out of sight of the camera, listening to the angry animal activists shouting slogans, when he felt himself picked up by the armpits and hauled to the end of the alleyway. He looked up to see a man in a collarless grey suit, with jet-black hair combed up into a Mohican. The man must have moved very quickly and quietly to have snuck up on him like that without being heard.

"Oi, you can't go picking up people and moving them!" protested Archie.

The man didn't respond. He had his back to Archie, blocking the entrance to the alleyway.

The door opened and Holly appeared with her

stepmum behind her. The grey man marched towards them. "Mrs Bigsby," he said, "I'm Weaver. The car is just up here."

Holly's stepmother tried not to stare at the man's hair. "Ah, thank you, Mr Weaver."

"Just Weaver. Is this child anything to do with you?" Weaver pointed at Archie.

"Hey, Archie," said Holly miserably.

"Yes, I think we better take them both back home if that's all right, er ... Weaver," replied Mrs Bigsby.

"Very good." The strange man pointed the keys at the car, unlocking it and opening the back door.

"Wow!" said Archie, peering inside.

"Wow!" repeated Holly.

Mrs Bigsby didn't say anything but it was obvious that she was thinking *wow!* too. Stepping into Brant Buchanan's Bentley was like entering a top-of-the-range, high-tech, futuristic living room. It had soft black leather seats, tinted windows, a plasma TV screen and rows of glowing red buttons along the doors, each one screaming out to be pressed. Weaver closed the door behind them and soft lighting came on.

"Don't touch anything," said Mrs Bigsby, sitting opposite them to keep her eye on them. Holly had never seen her look so angry.

The plasma screen behind the driver's seat where Weaver sat flickered to life and his unsmiling face appeared. "Could I take the young man's name, please?" he said.

"Archie Snellgrove," said Archie, fastening the seatbelt. "Why?"

"To find your address."

"It's OK. I'll just walk back from Holly's house," said Archie anxiously.

Weaver's face, which had been full-screen, shrunk into a small box in the corner. Archie's name appeared one letter at a time as Weaver typed it out. The cursor flickered and a map of London appeared. The picture zoomed in on South London where a small red car was flashing. There was a flag nearby with an address on it.

"Number seventy-eight Sidney Clavel Estate," read Weaver. "If you would like a drink, the button on your door has a selection."

"Cool," said Archie. He reached his hand out to

hit one of the glowing red buttons only for Weaver to say, "Better not press that one. We don't really need to summon the helicopter right now. Also, it would be better if you avoided pressing the one that calls the US President. The drinks are controlled by the row above."

Archie found the right row and pressed a button. Instantly the armrest between Holly and him twisted around and a glass of orange juice rose up.

"That's neat," said Holly. "I wonder what this one does."

She pressed another button, turning on soothing classical music.

Mrs Bigsby leaned forwards and snatched the glass of juice. "No more buttons." She took a sip. "You two are in enough trouble."

With the gentle melody of the violins and cellos, the smooth running of the car and the tinted windows, it was as though they were gliding invisibly through the world.

The luxury of the car interior was a stark contrast to the block of flats where Archie lived. A group of boys who had been kicking a ball against a wall stopped to stare as Weaver parked.

"Home sweet home," said Archie, opening the door. "See you tomorrow then?" he asked Holly as he stepped out.

"Holly won't be seeing anyone for the foreseeable future," stated Mrs Bigsby. "She's grounded."

"Grounded?" Holly exclaimed. "How long for?"

"For the rest of the summer."

"Oi, nice car!" shouted one of the boys. "Can I have a drive?"

"Hey, that's little smelly-grove," yelled another.

"I'll see you later then," said Archie, making a sudden dash across the lawn towards the block of flats on the far side.

The boys took chase, but Archie was quick and he beat them to the building, through the outer door and to the central staircase that led up to the flats.

As they drove away, Holly twisted round to look out of the back window. Archie ran along the top walkway to a green door. She could feel his panic as he pounded on the door until it opened. He dived inside with seconds to spare. The door slammed shut just as the boys arrived outside it. She didn't like to think what would have happened if they had caught him.

"Sit down properly," snapped her stepmum irritably.

Holly did as she was told and neither of them spoke for the rest of the journey.

When they arrived at the house, Weaver opened the door and Holly climbed out. Mrs Bigsby led her to the front door.

"Go to your room. I need to talk to your father in private."

Holly walked up the stairs, feeling miserable, frustrated and angry. In her bedroom, she sat on her bed and stared at the door. Tears built up in her eyes. She tried to hold them back but she couldn't help herself. Willow crawled out from under the bed and scrambled up on to the bed and into Holly's lap, offering a soft, comforting meow. Holly stroked her and wondered what she should do next.

In general, Mountain Dragons felt at home in wide open spaces where they were free to spread their wings, but Dirk Dilly wasn't most Mountain Dragons. London was his home. He felt safe there.

"I still do not understand why we are coming back to this big humano nest?" said Alba.

"You don't need to understand," said Dirk, landing on an old-fashioned red-brick library at a busy crossroads. "You need to keep quiet and stay close."

He stood on his hind legs to work out the best route.

"Excuse me, Mr Dirk, which way is the place called Deptford?"

"That direction," replied Dirk, pointing. "Why do you want to know that?"

"I am just a natural curiosity," she replied.

"Naturally curious," corrected Dirk. "Come on."

The lights changed and he leaped across the road. Alba made the jump and landed with a loud **THUD** on the roof.

"Frank, did you hear that? It sounded like something just landed on the roof," shouted a woman's voice.

"It's probably those blasted squirrels," another voice responded. "I'll get the broom."

"Will you be careful!" Dirk whispered angrily to Alba. He knew that Alba and London didn't mix well but he wished he had a way of shaking her off. He needed to look at that book. He hoped there was something in *Dragonlore* that would help him find a Sky Dragon and solve this case once and for all.

Dirk paused on a rooftop by a grassy roundabout near a row of shops. He looked down at the shoppers in the high street. Humanity's love of shopping had always fascinated him. It always looked to him like a kind of hobby that made people miserable. Big droplets of rain began to fall and the already disgruntled shoppers groaned and put up umbrellas.

The rain gave Dirk and Alba enough cover to move more quickly across the city. It wasn't long before they were soaring through Dirk's office window.

Inside, Dirk picked up the remote control, out of habit pointing it at the TV, before remembering that Alba had smashed it.

"What does it do, this box of light and noise?" asked Alba.

"It *was* a television," replied Dirk pointedly. "Before you broke it, it told me what was going on in the world," he said, even though he spent more time watching old detective films and reruns of cop shows than news programmes.

Looking around the room he realized that Mrs Klingerflim had tidied up. There was no sign of the book but on the desk was a note.

Mr Dilly,
I've gone out. I have tidied up and opened the window.
Don't worry about the rent. Oh, and I lent dear
Ivor's book to Holly. What a lovely girl. So polite.
    Yours,
    Mrs K.

"I've got to go out," said Dirk.

"I will be coming with you," said Alba.

"Not this time. The city isn't safe for you. You can't blend and you don't know these roofs like I do."

"But I must stay with you at all times."

"Listen to me, Alba. We will find the Sky Dragon and your sister, but I can't risk you going out there again. Besides, I've got to go and visit a humano. You wouldn't like that, would you?"

"Meet a humano? That would not be good."

"OK, so stay here," he replied. "Keep the blinds down and don't answer the door. If anyone knocks, I'm not in, you're not in, there's no one here, OK?"

"OK, I understand," said Alba. She picked up a tin of beans. "Can I eat some of your crunchy-shelled food?"

"Knock yourself out, but maybe avoid the bathroom products this time."

Across the road from Holly lived a nosy old woman who spent her days sitting by her window, behind her net curtains, watching every single event in Elliot

Drive and noting them down in her diary. If the man at forty-seven got an extra pint of milk delivered, or the lady at forty-one had a suspiciously long conversation with the postman, it went down in her diary.

She had noted that Holly hadn't left the house at all since she and her stepmother had been spotted stepping out of a very expensive-looking silver car on Saturday. A blond-haired boy had visited every day but had been sent away.

Had she only looked up at the roof that evening, she would have seen a medium-sized dragon squeeze its green belly through Holly's window. Luckily, she was too busy jotting down all of the number plates of the cars parked on the pavement.

Inside, Holly threw her arms around Dirk and hugged him. "Where have you been? I kept trying to call."

"I've been out of town on a case. That's why I'm here."

"So you didn't come to see me," said Holly, unable to hide her disappointment.

Dirk lifted her chin with his paw. "I'm sorry, kiddo,

I've been wrapped up in this case," he said.

"What's it about?" she replied.

"In four words: *Sky Dragon Kidnaps Sea Dragon*," said Dirk.

"That's five words," pointed out Holly.

"Yes, but two of them are the same word."

"So what are Sky Dragons like?" asked Holly.

"Most of the time they're like clouds," said Dirk.

"Clouds?" repeated Holly. "You mean dragon-shaped clouds—"

"Are dragons," Dirk finished her sentence. "Precisely. The problem is they've been living in the clouds for a long time. No one knows much about them. I was hoping I'd be able to find something that might help in Mrs K's book."

Holly looked down. "Oh."

"'Oh,' doesn't sound good."

"I haven't got it," Holly admitted. "It was confiscated."

"Do you know where it is?"

"Well... Yes."

"Fine, just tell me where and I'll swing by and grab it," said Dirk.

"It won't be that easy," said Holly.

"Come on." Dirk spread his paws and grinned. "Remember who you're talking to here."

"It's been confiscated by the seventh richest man in the world and is being kept in the upstairs office of a high-security animal experimentation lab in Kennington," said Holly.

Dirk laughed. "You've been busy, then?" he said.

Holly brought Dirk up to date with all that had happened over the last few days. She told him about Brant Buchanan, her stepmum accepting a job for Global Sands and the conversation she had overheard about the AOG Project.

"He must be after the earthquake creator," said Dirk.

"That's what I thought but why would a billionaire businessman want a weapon?"

"I can think of lots of reasons," he replied. "For a man like that, business *is* war. So how did he end up with the book?"

"I wanted to find out what they were up to, so I broke in but I got caught."

"They didn't see you blending, did they?"

"No, but they took away the book as a punishment."

"You think he knows what it is?" asked Dirk, nervous about a human with so much wealth and power possessing a book that told the truth about dragonkind.

"I don't think so. He just thinks it's a silly book for kids."

"Good. Talk me through the security."

Holly recounted everything Mr Buchanan had told her about the building and how she had got in with Archie's help.

Dirk thought for a moment. "We'll need a distraction," he said.

"Archie could help again," suggested Holly.

"No, the security guard might recognize him. Besides, I don't want any more humans knowing about me. We need someone the guard won't know, someone we can trust," said Dirk, looking at her with a knowing wink.

"I'll make the call," replied Holly, understanding instantly what he meant. "What time?"

Dirk looked up at Holly's wall clock. He scratched his head uncertainly.

"Here, try this," said Holly, showing him her watch.

He read the time. 19:01.

"Digital – so much easier," said Dirk, who had always struggled with the human concept of time.

"Tell him we need the distraction at a quarter to eight."

Holly nodded and went to make the phone call. As he waited, Dirk checked out her room. He had never been in it before. It was all very Holly. On her desk were bits of paper with pencil-drawn pictures. He picked one up and recognized it as himself. He pulled open a drawer and saw the Shade-Hugger claw that they had discovered on their last case together. Dirk had forgotten all about it. She must have held on to it. It was against Dragonlore to let a human have any evidence of dragon existence but if anyone could be trusted with it, it was Holly.

When she came back in, he said, "I'm sorry I never returned your call."

"That's OK," she said. "You're here now."

"Won't your parents come and check on you?"

"No. My dad's out and my stepmum has a friend coming round."

"Let's go then."

With Holly's arms wound tightly round his neck, Dirk scampered across the rows of residential roofs, expertly negotiating every aerial and chimney in his way. He jumped, flew and glided across South London, unseen by the human inhabitants glued to their screens of various sizes. He came to a sudden stop on a rooftop by the high street.

"There's a bus coming," he said. "Quick, blend with me."

Dragon and girl vanished from sight just as the bus stopped next to them. Its top deck was level with the roof where they were hiding.

The driver indicated left and began to pull out.

"That's the problem with buses," said Dirk. "The

top decks are ideal places for dragon-spotting. Now, hold on."

Dirk leaped off the roof, spread his wings and landed gently on top of the moving bus, gripping tightly with his claws.

The only person to spot him was an overweight advertising executive in his second-storey apartment across the road from the bus stop. The man had been trying out his new running machine, but he stopped running when he saw a dragon with a girl on its back land on a double decker bus. He rubbed his eyes and looked again to find the bus still there but the dragon and the girl gone. Deciding that exercise clearly didn't agree with him, he went downstairs to the kitchen where he found a large tub of strawberry-cheesecake-flavoured ice cream and a big spoon.

It wasn't the first time Dirk had been spotted as he carried out his day to day occupation as a London-based dragon detective, but humans' ability to disbelieve their own eyes had ensured that he always got away with these brief moments of visibility.

When the bus stopped outside the Global Sands building, Dirk flew over the silver gates and landed on the flat roof of the lab. He poked his head over the edge and looked through the window of the office.

"It's empty," he informed Holly.

She checked her watch. "It's almost time."

Dirk got into position and pulled out a black sphere about the size of a golf ball from behind his right wing.

"Hold this," he said, handing it to Holly.

"What is it?" she asked, inspecting it. She recognized it as the object she'd mistaken for a paperweight on Dirk's desk.

"It's a retroreflective camera-neutralizer. It sends invisible infrared lasers to block the security cameras."

"Where did you get it?"

"I found it," he replied, flicking out the claws on his right paw, checking the sharpness of each, then plunging them into the roof. With the claws on his left paw he began to cut a hole.

"Mr Buchanan said nothing could cut through this roof," said Holly.

"Buchanan has obviously never come across a dragon claw," said Dirk.

Once he had made the hole, he pulled the piece of

roof away. Carefully, he lifted one of the ceiling tiles of Brant Buchanan's office, revealing the room below, then he took the black sphere off Holly.

"Check if he's here yet," he said.

She crawled to the edge and looked over. In the alleyway, a man in a baseball cap was standing in front of the back door to the lab. The man checked his watch and swizzled his baseball cap around, revealing the well-worn face of Ladbroke Blake, the private detective who had once been hired to follow Holly and, ever since, helped her out whenever she needed him. That night, instead of his trench coat, he was wearing a lurid red puffa jacket and in his hands was a large pizza box. He glanced at his watch again, chucked a piece of gum into his mouth and pressed the intercom buzzer at precisely 19:45.

"Aye?" Hamish's voice came through the intercom.

"Free pizza, mate?" said Ladbroke, chewing the gum, speaking in a strong cockney accent.

"I didn't order a pizza."

"Nah, mate, it's part of one of them promotional campaigns. It's free. That's why I called it a free pizza. So do you want it or not?"

"I can't go opening this door for a free pizza. I've got my job to think about here, laddie," said Hamish.

"Fair enough, chum. I'll see if anyone else wants this free haggis pizza then."

"Did you say haggis pizza?" said Hamish, suddenly sounding interested.

"Yeah, it's one of our specials, sounds disgusting if you ask me. What is haggis, anyway? Smells pretty grim."

"Philistine," said Hamish. "Haggis is the food of the gods. I've never had it on a pizza, mind... And I *am* a bit peckish. Stay there, I'm coming now."

Ladbroke glanced around. On the phone Holly hadn't told him where she would be or why she needed him to act as a distraction, and he hadn't asked. Holly always got the feeling that Ladbroke Blake had seen a lot more of the world than most people.

She nodded at Dirk and he dropped the camera-neutralizer into the room below them, waited for a second or two, then jumped in after it.

He landed in a crouching position and quickly took in the layout of the office. Behind him was the glass desk. In front was the purple sofa. There was a door to his right and on the ceiling were three cameras. He hoped the camera-neutralizer was working, otherwise the security cameras would be recording his every move.

Holly's head appeared through the hole in the roof.

Dirk straightened up, grabbed her, then lowered her into the room.

"We need to be quick," he said.

"The book's in there," said Holly, pointing to the copy of *Dragonlore*, clearly visible in the transparent desk's drawer. She tried to open it, only to find it locked.

"I'll have to pick the lock," said Dirk. "Go and keep watch."

Following orders didn't come very naturally to Holly but it was different with Dirk. She trusted him.

She made her way down the stairs. At the bottom she stopped – she could hear footsteps. She looked through a glass pane in the door and saw the slim grey figure of Weaver striding down the corridor. She watched him walk into the room full of animal cages. Intrigued, she crept into the corridor and peered through the window that looked into the room.

The bright overhead lighting flickered on and she saw Weaver carrying a plastic container with air holes along the top. He placed the container on a counter and pulled out what appeared to be a remote control from his pocket. He pressed a button. The container opened automatically and six white mice filed out, each walking to its designated cage. They were wearing the same metallic collars she had seen on the tabby cat.

Holly was suddenly distracted by a door at the other end of the corridor opening. She saw the edge of a silver case and then a mobile phone rang.

"Hello?" It was Brant Buchanan.

Holly took her chance, slipping out of the corridor and back up the stairs without being seen.

Dirk pushed the tip of his smallest claw into the keyhole and jiggled it about. Picking locks was a fiddly business. Eventually he heard the click of the drawer being unlocked but, before he could grab the book, the door burst open and Holly entered.

"Hide!" she whispered. "Buchanan's coming. There's no time to get out."

Holly ran to the side of the couch and Dirk dived into the corner by the desk. They both blended with their surroundings as the door opened.

From his position on the floor, Dirk watched Brant Buchanan cross the room. He placed the silver case on the desk, pulled up a chair and sat down.

Through the glass, Dirk could read three letters on the base of the case: AOG.

"Hello, this is Hamish Fraser on security." The voice came through the intercom.

"Yes, Hamish?" replied Buchanan.

"Is everything all right up there, Mr Buchanan, sir? The security cameras are out."

"Everything's fine, thank you."

"Right then. Sorry to bother you."

As Buchanan released the button on the intercom, he noticed that his desk drawer was unlocked. He pulled it open and lifted out the red book with the white zigzag on the cover.

For a few moments they all sat in silence while Buchanan flicked through the book, then he pressed the intercom again.

"Weaver, get up here," he said.

"Yes, sir," replied the voice.

Holly had seen how quickly Weaver could move but she was still impressed by how quickly he dropped what he was doing and ran up the stairs. The man marched into the room, his grey eyes twitching and alert.

"What is it, sir?"

"Ah, Weaver, listen to this," said Buchanan. "'Snow Dragons are one of the biggest challenges to a dragon spotter,'" the billionaire read aloud. "'Not only do they live in the furthermost regions of Antarctica but, being both white-bellied and white-backed, they are incredibly well camouflaged. If you are lucky and do get close enough to see one in detail you will notice that the underbelly is covered in a very fine fur. This provides excellent insulation against the cold.'"

"Er... Very interesting, sir," said Weaver, not sounding at all interested.

"Did you believe in dragons when you were a child, Weaver?" Buchanan asked.

"I can't remember, sir."

"I did. It sounds stupid but I believed that the world was full of dragons. Only they were in hiding, waiting for the right time to attack us. The funny thing was, I wasn't scared. Do you know why?"

"No, sir."

"Because for some reason I believed they would be on my side."

"Yes, sir," said Weaver. "Can we deal with the matter in hand now?"

"It's always work, work, work with you, Weaver." Buchanan sighed.

"I'm sorry, sir. But I think this is rather more pressing than fairy stories about made-up creatures."

"As usual, you are completely right," admitted his boss. "Show me how this thing works."

Weaver reached over the desk, his grey shoes stepping dangerously close to Dirk's nose, and pressed buttons on either side of the silver case. It opened but Dirk couldn't see what it said on the screen.

"Normally it requires the Prime Minister's DNA authentication to operate," Weaver explained. "Fortunately, because of the recent government change, we have acquired it during a handover period."

"Meaning?"

"Anyone who knows how to use it can operate it."

"And do we know how to use it?" Buchanan asked.

"Yes. It came with instructions." Weaver smiled and dropped a pamphlet on the desk.

Dirk read the cover:

AOG PROJECT

NAPOW TECHNOLOGY

THE VE 6.2 OPERATING MANUAL

TOP SECRET

"How very considerate of our friends in the Ministry of Defence," said Buchanan.

"I'm sorry to bother you again, sir." Hamish's voice came through the intercom. "You've got a visitor. Angela Bigsby."

"Thank you, send her up."

"Are you sure this is wise? We barely know her," said Weaver, pacing anxiously.

"Relax. She's on the payroll. She's one of us now," said Buchanan.

The door opened and Holly's stepmum entered.

"Ah, Angela," said Buchanan, a broad grin on his face. "Look what we have here."

Mrs Bigsby looked at the silver case on the desk. "But... But..." she stammered. "H-how did you, er, acquire it so quickly?"

"You don't need to get bogged down in the details. The fact is we have what we want and it's all thanks to you."

"You promised no one would get hurt…" said Mrs Bigsby, sounding more nervous than Holly had ever heard her sound.

"I'm not a monster," said Brant.

"But the ministry will be looking for it, won't they?"

Buchanan laughed. "Angela, you should know yourself that when something as top secret as this goes missing, usual procedure is to deny that it exists at all. Looking for it draws too much attention."

"Yes, that is true," admitted Mrs Bigsby.

Buchanan turned to Weaver. "By the way, Weaver, good thinking knocking the security cameras out. You can't be too careful."

"I haven't done anything to the cameras," said Weaver, a sharp edge of anxiety in his voice.

"But Hamish said that they were—" Buchanan stopped mid-flow.

"You should get out of here," said Weaver urgently. "I'll do a proper sweep of the building but you need to leave immediately."

"You worry too much, Weaver. It's probably just a glitch. You know what technology is like, even our own."

"All the same. Please, sir," said Weaver firmly.

"All right. Come on, Angela, I'll give you a lift home," said Buchanan, standing up. "We can discuss your role at Global Sands on the way."

Weaver escorted his boss and Mrs Bigsby to the car, then went back into the building alone. He systematically checked each camera. The red lights were on, which meant there was no fault with the equipment itself. He searched Buchanan's office and discovered a small black sphere about the size of a golf ball. He picked it up and inspected it.

"Interesting," he said to himself, dropping it into his pocket.

He walked to the desk and noticed that the instructions for the VE 6.2 and the red book with the white zigzag were no longer there.

"Very interesting," he said, dropping to his knees and inspecting the floor. He found an area where the thick green carpet had been flattened. He jumped up with his arms outstretched and knocked the ceiling tile directly above it away. Where there should have been solid roof, there was a hole revealing the evening sky.

Weaver grabbed the chair from behind the desk, placed it below the hole and used it to climb out on to the roof. He scanned the rooftops and streets for any sign of the intruder, but whoever it was had gone. He looked closely at the jagged piece of roof that had been cut away.

"Extremely interesting," he said, dropping back down into the office.

19

Dirk stopped a couple of streets from his office on the flat roof of a kebab shop with a good view of his window. The light was on and the blinds were pulled down.

"Aren't we going in?" asked Holly.

"No, Alba will freak out if she sees you. And don't you want to know what that silver case does first?"

Holly slipped off his back and opened the instruction manual Dirk had stolen. "The VE 6.2 is the latest weapon to come from the AOG project. VE stands for Volcano Erupter. It uses the same sonar technology as the QC3000 to cause any targeted volcano in the world to suddenly erupt regardless of how dormant it is believed to be."

"Another triumph for the AOG project," said Dirk grimly.

"Why would anyone want a volcano to erupt?" asked Holly.

"Nature's weapons are the most powerful," said Dirk. "Volcanoes can wipe out entire cities, they can destabilize economies, create confusion and fear. And unlike conventional attacks, there's no one to retaliate against."

"At least we have the instructions," said Holly.

"True," agreed Dirk. "Now for Sky Dragons."

He pulled out the copy of *Dragonlore* and turned to the relevant chapter, flicking quickly through the pages until he found what he was looking for. Holly read it over his shoulder.

Spotting Sky Dragons

Of all the breeds, the Sky Dragon is both the most commonly spotted dragon in the world (what child hasn't identified one in the sky?) as well as being the most mysterious. The author of this book is disappointed to inform you that, in spite of countless hours spent searching, he has never seen one in solid form.

It is thought that Sky Dragons often travel in vast herds, communicating with each other using a type of telepathy beyond the reach of other dragons. These herds have often been the source of confusion for meteorologists and the cause of many incorrect predictions of rain.

Although they rarely appear in any form other than that of passing clouds, some believe that one way to make them appear involves another dragon spitting liquid fire from the Earth's Outer Core directly into the heart of a sublimated Sky Dragon, forcing it to materialize.

"I should get back to Alba," said Dirk.

"It looks like she isn't waiting around for you," said Holly, pointing to his office window, where the blind was now up and there was a large shadow blocking the light. The shadow shifted and the Sea Dragon jumped out of the window, landing on the roof across the road, sending a few slates crashing to the ground.

"Rats at a disco," groaned Dirk. "What's she up to?"

"I don't know," replied Holly, "but I think she may have come face to face with a human being now."

On Alba's back, arms around her neck, was a boy.

"It's Archie," she said.

"Your new friend?" replied Dirk.

"Yeah, but how—" started Holly.

"I don't know," interrupted Dirk, "but they seem to be in a hurry. Come on."

Following Alba was made harder by the trail of destruction she left in her wake. Dirk had his work cut out to avoid being spotted by the humans wondering what had knocked their aerials off their roofs.

The darkness helped hide his movements, but Dirk was relieved when Alba finally came to a standstill on the corrugated roof of a hut inside a yard full of beaten-up old cars. Dirk stopped on a nearby factory, keeping his distance. He looked around for an indication of where they were.

"Interesting," mused Dirk.

"What is?" asked Holly.

"We're in Deptford," said Dirk. "Alba asked me about Deptford. I'm beginning to wonder whether this whole thing hasn't been an act. Something's going on and I don't like it. Not one bit."

Holly and Dirk were surprised to discover Archie riding on Alba's back, but it was nothing compared to the astonishment Archie was feeling. He had knocked on Holly's door every day since Saturday only to be turned away. On the last of these visits, Mrs Bigsby had hissed, "This incessant harassment must cease," and slammed the door.

Archie didn't want to cease anything. If calling for Holly was out of the question, then he would have to pursue other means. Then he remembered what Holly had said about her uncle being a detective. Archie had gone to the library, found a spare computer and typed in 'Dirk Dilly' and 'detective'. After a little scrolling and a couple of dead ends, he had found a review written by a Carolyn Rosenfield recommending a private investigating service called *The Dragon Detective Agency*.

"Cool name," Archie had muttered to himself as he typed this into the search engine. The name had led to a phone number, which he committed to memory. Back at home, he had called it. On the first three attempts, the phone rang out. But on the third attempt, someone did pick up.

"Please stop the ring ring, Aforrn," said a female Spanish-accented voice.

"Er, what?" said Archie.

"Oh, hello? Is someone inside this thing?"

"I wanted to speak to Dirk Dilly," said Archie. "I'm a friend of his niece's. I was hoping he could help me."

"Oh, you mean, you're one of *our kind*," said Alba. "He is helping me too. Although now, I have been left here and I have eaten all of the crunchy bean fruit."

"Ri-ight," said Archie uncertainly. "Now, where are you?"

"Inside and upstairs."

"You might need to be more specific. You don't know the name of the road?"

"Only the wall," replied Alba.

"What wall?"

"The wall outside is called Ivydale Road. The door

140

below is called 382. Is that a funny name for a door? We do not have doors where I come from."

It didn't take Archie long to get there and, before long, he was standing outside informing the white-haired old lady who answered it that he was a friend of Holly's and there to speak to Mr Dilly.

"I don't think he's in," she said.

Upstairs a loud **CRASH** rocked the whole building.

"Although I could be wrong," she added, with a little wink. "Let's go and see. Holly's told you about Mr Dilly, has she?"

"Oh yes, we're best friends, we don't have any secrets," Archie said, following her upstairs.

"Mr Dilly," she called, knocking on the door. "Are you in, Mr Dilly?'

There was a pause then the same voice from the phone said, "I am not in, Mr Dilly is not in, there is no one here."

Alba recoiled in fear as the handle turned and she watched the door open. She tried to hide under the desk but, in her hurry, missed and whacked her head against the corner.

"Ouch!" She rubbed her head and found herself staring at two humans. The elderly female was smiling but the young male was staring, utterly gobsmacked.

"Er, is that a dragon?" asked Archie.

"To be precise, she's a grey-backed, blue-bellied Sea Dragon," replied Mrs Klingerflim. "Possibly Portuguese?"

"Hu... Hu... Humanos," Alba stammered.

"Actually, she sounds Spanish," said Mrs Klingerflim.

"I am breaching the forbidden divide," wailed Alba, trying to hide behind a newspaper but accidentally tearing it in two.

"Ivor and I used to spot Sea Dragons off the coast of Wales," said Mrs Klingerflim fondly.

"You knew there was a dragon in your house?" said Archie, staring at the old lady with as much astonishment as he had looked at Alba.

"Oh yes, but I didn't know there was a *Sea* Dragon up here," she said, approaching Alba to inspect her more closely. "Do you mind if I feel your back?"

"Stay away from me," said Alba, edging backwards.

Mrs Klingerflim stroked Alba's tail and said, "You feel like you've been out of the sea for just over a week. Is that right?"

"How is a humano knowing so much about our kind?" said Alba accusingly.

"My dear Ivor used to love Sea Dragons," she replied. "Sky Dragons have always been my favourite, though."

"You know about Sky Dragons?"

"Oh yes, Ivor hated not being able to see them properly but that just made them more interesting to me. In fact, I ended up writing the chapter on them."

"Do you know how I could be finding one?" asked Alba.

"Since you *are* a dragon, you could always try summoning it," suggested Mrs Klingerflim.

"How can I be doing this?"

"As I recall, you have to fire liquid fire from the Outer Core into its heart. Sounds like a terrible to-do to me."

Alba tilted her head to one side, digesting what she was being told. "This really works?"

"I don't know for sure," said Mrs Klingerflim. "I've never had the chance to test it. You can't exactly buy liquid fire from the chemist."

"I have some," said Alba. "I have some in a flask." She showed them.

"Yes, but why would you *want* to summon a Sky Dragon?" asked Mrs Klingerflim.

"That's just what I was going to ask," said Archie, who had adjusted to the fact he was talking to a dragon and loving every minute of it.

"I must go to Deptford," said Alba.

"Of course." Archie grinned. "Where else would

a dragon go? Hey, I can show you the way. My dad used to have a business down that way."

Alba shrank away as Archie approached. "It would be very bad to carry a humano."

"Not this one. I'm like a lucky penny. Ask anyone."

Alba thought for a moment before responding. "This is more important to me than the forbidden divide so I am deciding to let you show me the way."

"Cool." Archie climbed on to the desk and jumped on to the dragon's back.

"Ouch, you are kicking me."

"Sorry. My name's Archie, by the way."

"And you can call me Alba Longs."

"How lovely," said Mrs Klingerflim, with a wistful glint in her eye. "If I was twenty years younger I'd be coming along but I don't have the hips for riding dragons these days."

She opened the window and took a step back, allowing Alba to leap out of the office.

"This is the coolest thing ever!" said Archie, gazing at the reddening sunset.

"Which way is the way?" asked Alba, before losing her footing on a solar panel, sliding down, then hopping to the next building.

"Be careful," said Archie as her tail sent an aerial flying. "Head for that pub at the end of the street but mind the—"

His words were cut short by Alba knocking over a row of chimney tops like they were skittles.

As they made their way across the rooftops of London, leaving a trail of destruction in their wake, neither of them noticed that they were being followed.

They had been travelling for around half an hour when they arrived at a breaker's yard on a road full of industrial estates and factories. Alba landed on the tin roof of a shack inside the yard. Battered cars were stacked up. There were piles of engines, exhausts, tyres and other car parts strewn around the place.

"You must get off here," said Alba.

Archie climbed off her back and pulled a jelly bean covered in fluff from his pocket.

"Here." He offered it to her.

"What is this small coloured pebble?" she asked cautiously.

"A jelly bean," replied Archie. "It's food."

"Food? I am starving," said Alba, taking it from his hand and throwing it into her mouth. Her eyes widened with delight. "This is delicious. I very like this jelly bean. Better than soap. Have you more?"

Archie rummaged in his pocket and pulled out another.

"I do not know how to be thanking you for these jelly beans but I must go and help my sister now. Thank you, Mr Archie," she said, jumping down into the yard and prowling around, peering into gutted cars, looking for something.

A male voice called out, "In here!"

Alba looked around, confused.

"I think it came from that truck," said Archie, pointing at a reddish-coloured vehicle by the gates.

Alba looked at the truck. The back doors were open. "Thank you, little humano," she whispered, walking cautiously up the ramp into the back.

"Hello?" she called. "Who is in there?"

The back doors of the truck suddenly swung shut, trapping Alba inside. The engine started. Archie tried to see who was in the driver's seat but the angle was no good. The truck reversed, backing into the gates and pushing them wide open, before swinging into the road.

Archie felt the corrugated iron roof buckle under the weight of something landing on it with such force that it knocked him off his feet. He looked up to see another dragon. This one had a green underbelly and a red back, and ears rather than gills. Its yellow eyes peered at him, then it spoke.

"So this is your friend, is it, Holly?"

Holly's head appeared over the dragon's shoulder. "Dirk Dilly meet Archie Snellgrove," she said.

Archie lowered his voice. "There's another dragon…" he said.

"I know. This is Dirk," said Holly, sliding off Dirk's back.

"There's another dragon…" repeated Archie.

"No kidding," said Dirk. "Where did Alba go? We lost sight of her. What was that truck doing?"

"I mean, there's *another* dragon…" he said for a third time.

"Your friend appears to be stuck on repeat," said Dirk. "It's probably shock."

"No," insisted Archie, speaking through his teeth.

"Another one. Down there."

Dirk turned to see what Archie was looking at. A brown-backed, caramel-bellied Shade-Hugger stepped out of the shell of a once-white van, covering his eyes from the last rays of daylight.

"Double-crossing rats," muttered Dirk.

"Karnataka," said Holly.

"Do you know all the dragons in London?" asked Archie, turning to Holly.

"All the ones worth knowing, yes," replied Holly simply.

21

Dirk flew down from the roof and landed on Karnataka's back. He caught him by surprise but Karnataka wriggled free and the two dragons squared off. Watching from the roof, Archie let out a whistle of admiration.

"Cool uncle!" he said.

"You can't tell anyone," replied Holly.

"Who would believe me?"

In the yard below, jagged jaws snapped, sharp talons swiped and buckets of grey smoke gushed from the huge nostrils of the battling dragons. Dirk pounced, knocking Karnataka off guard and pinning him to the ground.

"I'm Dragnet Captain now," whined Karnataka.

"You can't do this. I order you to release me."

"Order me? You're getting ideas above your station," replied Dirk. "All this power has gone to your—"

His words were cut short as a metal cuff slammed shut around his neck. A sudden jolt brought his head into the side of a rusty Ford Capri.

"I think you'll find my station exactly matches my ideas, these days." Karnataka stood up and brushed himself down. "Good work, Officer Grunling." He turned to Dirk and said, "Balti here is my most trusted officer."

Dirk pulled his head out of the dent it had made in the car door to see the dirt-brown Drake, Balti Grunling.

"Oh, it's you," said Balti to Dirk. "You owe me pepper."

Dirk remembered that he had bribed Balti the last time they met with the promise of some pepper to liven up his otherwise rather plain mud diet.

"I'll get you all the pepper you need if you let me go," Dirk said.

Balti dragged Dirk's head into the car again, making the dent bigger, then he puffed out his chest and said, "Assaulting Captain Karnataka the Fearless is an extremely serious offence. Shall I read him his rights, sir?"

"Not just yet," said Karnataka. "I need to speak to him in private. Leave us. I'll call when I need you."

"I'm sorry, sir," said Balti pompously, "but that would be most irregular. This criminal attacked you."

"As your captain, I order you to give me that chain and leave. This dragon and I have business," said Karnataka.

"Well, it's very unorthodox," grumbled Officer Grunling, begrudgingly unhooking the chain from his tail and handing it to his superior. He waddled over to a small mound of rock, where he muttered something and disappeared into the ground.

Crouching on the roof above, Archie whispered to Holly, "Where did he go?"

"The rock took him down," said Holly. "We need to help Dirk."

"Why? I thought he said they were friends," said Archie, although, watching Karnataka swing Dirk around on the chain, they didn't exactly look very friendly.

"We need to help him," said Holly, looking for a safe way down from the roof of the shack.

Karnataka pounced on Dirk. "Spill the beans, Dirk," he said in his nasal whine. "You've found out, haven't you?"

"What beans? Found out what?" said Dirk, struggling to breathe.

"How to contact a Sky Dragon, of course."

Karnataka had dragged Dirk's head so far back that Dirk was looking at him upside down. The angle was incredibly painful and not the most attractive view of Karnataka. Dirk could see right up his nose. So it was with great relief that Dirk watched a wing mirror smash into the side of Karnataka's face.

"Ow!" exclaimed the Shade-Hugger. Dirk took the opportunity to twist round and send a mouthful of fire at Karnataka. Karny screeched in pain and Dirk jumped up, landing on top of him. He glanced up to see Holly and Archie standing nearby, poised with more bits of car to fling at his signal.

"Thanks!" Dirk called to them.

"No problem," replied Holly.

Dirk reached behind Karnataka's wing and retrieved a key hidden there. He undid the neck cuff, while holding Karny down with his other three sets of claws.

"Let me go," said Karnataka.

"First things first," replied Dirk. "How do you know that I'm looking for a Sky Dragon?"

"How? I... I... I'll tell you how. It's my job to know these things, that's h-how," stammered Karnataka nervously.

"But if you knew about the Sky Dragons that means—" Dirk stopped mid-flow. Something clicked into place. "You set the whole thing up, didn't you, Karny?"

"I don't know what you mean," said Karnataka, trying to avoid his gaze.

"You sent Alba to find me and lead me to her sister's cave. The ash outline wasn't real, was it? The idea was to make me think her sister's disappearance had something to do with a Sky Dragon. Shute was right. No Sky Dragon has materialized in hundreds of years. You tricked me. I'll bet Alba doesn't even have a sister."

Karnataka writhed, trying to get free, but Dirk held him firmly.

"Delfina is real enough," said Karnataka, "real and in prison, arrested by Officer Grunling on some trumped up charge of spying for the Kinghorns. You know how overzealous these Drakes can be with their arrests. When Alba came to me to plead for her release I came up with the plan to get her to hire you. I knew that your first stop would be the last place her sister was seen and that you'd find the outline of ash I made in her cave and assume that a Sky Dragon was responsible for her disappearance. Then it was only a matter of time before you found out how to contact the Sky Dragons."

"That two-faced, lying Sea Dragon…" snarled Dirk.

"Don't be too hard on her. I told her that if she failed I would banish Delfina with the other Kinghorn traitors. She was only trying to save her sister – save her from the Inner Core."

"Why Sky Dragons?" asked Dirk.

"The Kinghorns are rising, Dirk," replied Karnataka. "They're waiting for the right time to attack. If we don't stop them it will be war – dragons against humans. The Drakes are tough enough but they haven't got the brains or power to defeat Vainclaw's army. Besides, offer them a big enough bribe and they'll swap sides before you can say liquorice laces. We need allies, Dirk. We need the Skies on our side. You've heard the stories; they have powers beyond any of us. *Firewalls*, Dirk."

Angry smoke poured from Dirk's nostrils. "Why involve me?"

"Because I knew you could find the answer but I also knew if I asked you directly, you wouldn't help me."

"You were right about that," Dirk snapped.

"Alba was supposed to meet me here as soon as she learned how to contact a Sky Dragon. I just got word from Balti that she was here. So where is she?"

"She got in a truck and it drove away," said Archie.

Karnataka looked at the blond-haired boy. "More kids, Dirk? Really?"

"This one wasn't my fault," he replied. He turned to Archie. "You mean she was in that truck we saw leave?"

"Yes, someone called her in and it drove off."

"Where's the truck going, Karny?"

"I don't know anything about a truck. She was supposed to meet me here in exchange for her sister's release."

"But if the truck is nothing to do with you…" began Dirk, his words trying to keep up with his racing thoughts. "Who else knows about this place?"

"No one, just me and the Drake."

Dirk swung his head around to address Archie again. "What did the truck look like?" he asked.

"It was sort of reddish-coloured," he replied.

"Anything else?"

"Only the two letters printed on the side."

"What two letters?"

"G and S."

"Global Sands!" gasped Holly.

"Rats on a stick!" exclaimed Dirk.

"Do you think Brant Buchanan really does know about dragons?" said Holly.

"I'm worried that it's looking that way," said Dirk. "Right, Captain Karnataka the Fearless, a Sea Dragon has been kidnapped by humans. It's time for you to live up to your name."

"Ah, well ... yes, right," mumbled Karnataka, edging away. "These days I have to follow correct Dragnet procedure. I'll alert the nearest duty officer who will assemble an emergency action committee meeting."

Dirk shot a burst of fire at him. "If you don't help me I'll go before the Dragon Council and tell them what I know about those missing Welsh gold reserves."

Karnataka could tell Dirk wasn't joking. "All right," he sighed. "What do you want me to do?"

"Take the boy with you and search east. We'll look west."

"You want me to carry a human? Are you mad?"

"While I'm chatting to the Council, I could also mention this little Sky Dragon scheme of yours. I wonder how they'll view your actions," added Dirk.

"But Dirk ... a human!" protested Karnataka. "I'm the captain of the Dragnet!"

"He'll help you identify the truck and you should have thought about that before you set me up," said Dirk.

Karnataka looked warily at Archie. "All right, get

on," he said, "but no kicking."

Archie climbed on. "Another dragon ride," he said. "This day just keeps getting better."

"Whoever finds the truck first sends up a fire flare to let the other know where he is," ordered Dirk. "Now let's get going."

Both dragons flew to the roof of the shack, Holly on Dirk's back, Archie on Karnataka's.

"And don't even think about ditching the kid and heading underground," warned Dirk. "It looks as though one of the most powerful humans on the planet has kidnapped a Sea Dragon. If we fail to rescue Alba, you can kiss goodbye to your cushy job as captain and say hello to full-scale war, dragons versus humans."

There were a surprisingly large number of reddish-coloured trucks in London that evening. Dirk and Holly searched the streets, but each time they thought they had spotted a truck that fitted the description, they would get close, only to find it wasn't the one they were looking for. It wasn't until they reached Waterloo that Holly saw one with the letters G and S printed in white on the side.

"That's it!" she said.

"It's heading for the bridge," Dirk pointed out. He took a deep breath and looked up at the sky. Holly struggled to cling on.

"What are you doing?" she asked, feeling his stomach swell.

He exhaled suddenly and Holly felt the skin around his neck get warm as a small fleck of light shot from his mouth.

"It's a fire flare," explained Dirk, "to show Karnataka where we are."

"Will he see it?" asked Holly, peering up into the sky, where the tiny pellet was barely visible.

"Keep watching," replied Dirk.

All of a sudden, the burning ember exploded in the sky. The Londoners who noticed it briefly paused to wonder who was letting off fireworks, then carried on doing whatever they had been doing.

"The truck's getting away," said Holly, seeing that it was already halfway across the bridge.

Dirk looked down. Jumping the river was always the most challenging part of his life in London, but it was dark and he had no choice but to risk it.

"Hold tight." Dirk took a small step back, then sprang up, flying high over the river. He landed on the first building on the other side and ran across the roof, vaulting over a line of stone figures. Across the rooftops he kept up with the truck as it drove through London's bustling streets.

"Why would they be taking a dragon further into London?" asked Holly.

"That's not the only question that needs answering. What about how would Buchanan know where Alba was meeting Karnataka in the first place?" said Dirk.

The truck eventually began to pull into an underground car park. Before they followed it in, Holly looked around to see they were next to an ugly skyscraper that towered above the surrounding buildings.

"Get ready to blend." Dirk jumped from a church to the roof of a pub, then to the top of the truck just before it went below ground.

"Oh no," murmured Dirk. "Height restriction."

A yellow sign in the entrance stated the maximum height allowed into the car park. There was barely enough room for the truck, let alone the extra passengers on top. Holly rolled off Dirk and lay flat as the truck drove in. As it entered the building, the sign scraped across Dirk's tough, ridged back, actually doing more damage to the sign than it did to him.

The truck trundled down to the lowest level and then came to a standstill. The car park had dim lights along the walls and concrete pillars that cast long shadows. Except for the truck, the entire level was empty.

Holly heard two people step out. Neither spoke as they slammed the doors shut and walked to the back of the truck, their footsteps echoing. Their features were shrouded by darkness, but as they opened the back doors and stepped into the light, Holly finally saw their faces. It was the pair of crooks, Arthur and Reg.

Something was stirring inside the truck. The long head of a dragon emerged, a thin line of smoke from its nostrils drifting up, making Holly's nose itch. She stifled a sneeze. Alba Longs stepped out.

"What's going on?" Holly whispered to Dirk.

Dirk motioned to stay quiet and they watched the two crooks silently escort the Sea Dragon across the car park into a lift.

"I'm going after them," said Dirk. "You should stay here. This could prove dangerous."

"I don't care. I'm coming with you," insisted Holly, climbing on to his back.

"There's no time to argue," said Dirk.

"Exactly, so let's go," she urged.

Dirk sprang from the roof of the truck and flew across the car park to the lift. He extended two claws, jammed them into the gap between the doors and strained as he pulled them wide open to reveal the empty elevator shaft. He pushed himself and Holly inside and the doors slammed shut again. It was dark inside. Above, they could hear the lift rapidly ascending.

"Hold tight," said Dirk. The shaft wasn't quite wide enough to spread his wings and fly up, so he half flew, half scampered, using the ladder that ran up the side to propel himself faster. They were gaining on the moving lift but Holly was being thrown about by Dirk, her legs flailing like a rag doll no matter how tightly she locked her arms around his neck.

"Don't lose me!" she yelled desperately.

"I won't!" shouted Dirk above the squeaks of the lift. He tried to use his tail to secure her to his back, but lost his rhythm and collided with a wall just as Holly's left leg was outstretched. There was a CRUNCH and Holly yelped in pain.

"Hang on," said Dirk, flapping one wing, giving

him enough of a final boost to grab on to the bottom of the lift, which was still hurtling upwards. He spun round, bringing himself face to face with Holly, so he was hanging upside down with her lying on his soft green underbelly.

"How are you doing, kid?" he asked.

Holly tried to smile but the pain turned it into a grimace.

The lift jolted violently as it reached the top of the shaft. Above them they heard footsteps as Alba and the crooks walked out.

Dirk jammed his claws into the underside of the lift, cutting straight through the base. He pulled one claw free and punched the metal until it bent back, making a hole big enough to climb through, then he hauled them both into the lift.

Dirk placed Holly on the floor as gently as possible. Her jeans were stained with sticky red blood. She winced in pain as he examined her leg.

"I'm so sorry," he said.

"Will it heal with sleep?" she asked, sucking her teeth.

"Not this time, Hol," he replied. "The bone's broken."

Holly had never felt such agony.

"We need to get you to a hospital," said Dirk.

"There's no time," she replied, her voice weak with pain.

Dirk knew she was right. The unfolding drama wasn't exactly going to pause and wait for them to deal with a broken leg. He hated to see Holly in such pain but he had no choice.

"Stay out of sight. I won't be long," said Dirk. He pressed the button to open the doors, then stepped out.

Alone in the lift, Holly examined her leg. It was the same one that Vainclaw Grandin, the leader of the Kinghorns, had slashed in Little Hope. She wondered how she was going to explain a broken leg to her parents.

She looked around for something to distract her from the pain. Above her was a row of buttons, each with a company name next to the corresponding floor. She twisted herself around to get a better look, lifting herself on her hands, trying to avoid putting any weight on the broken leg. At the top she could see 'GS' in block capitals on a red background, just like the one on the truck. Below it was the full company name in smaller writing. She strained to read it but it was a tricky angle. She remembered how on the Global Sands website every division used the same logo of a dark blue GS in a circle. It seemed strange that here in the lift and on the truck were the only times she had seen it written differently.

She pushed herself up the wall, bashing her leg and sending a spasm of pain rattling through her body. She tried again, this time raising herself high enough to read the tiny writing. It didn't say Global Sands. The company name was Gronkong Shinard.

She had heard the name somewhere before but

she couldn't quite place where. As she was trying to figure out why it sounded so familiar, she felt the lift move and lost her footing. Landing on her bad leg, she narrowly avoided slipping through the hole Dirk had made in the floor. The lift juddered again – it was going down.

Dirk followed a few stairs to a door that led to the roof of the skyscraper. The sounds of the London evening drifted up from the streets. Alba Longs stood on her hind legs with her back to him. The two crooks were on either side of her, holding a large net. Neither of them looked at Dirk.

"I am not sure I can do it," said Alba.

"You must do what we say," said Arthur.

"No one need get hurt," added Reg.

"Are these two gentlemen bothering you, Alba?" asked Dirk casually.

They all spun around to look at him. Alba was holding the flask that Shute Hobcraft had given her.

"Mr Dilly! You must go or—"

"Alba. Leave this to me," interrupted Dirk. Without

warning, he sprang into action, spinning horizontally through the air towards the unwitting crooks, using his tail to send both men staggering backwards. He yanked the net from their hands and threw it over their heads, bagging both of them. Dirk lifted the net to look at them squashed together inside.

"That was easy," said Dirk.

"Oww," said Reg. "What's going on? The last thing I remember, we were bagging leaves."

"Judging by our current predicament I think we may have died and been reincarnated as fish," replied Arthur, who was facing the other way and hadn't yet seen Dirk.

"We're in the sky," said Reg, also unaware of the dragon holding the net.

"Flying fish, perhaps," said Arthur.

"Dragonsong," snarled Dirk.

He shook the net, banging the two villains' heads together and knocking them out. "Someone hypnotized them with Dragonsong. Did you do this, Alba?"

He turned on her, angry smoke billowing from his nostrils.

"I would never," wailed Alba. "I only wanted to help my sister."

"What are you talking about? Karnataka has Delfina locked up. I know you've been lying to me."

"You are right," said Alba, averting her eyes. "I have spoken untruths but I am not the liar now. Delfina is no longer in the prison."

"Where is she then?" demanded Dirk.

Behind him he heard the *ting!* of the lift door opening. He turned around to see smoke billowing out like the lift had caught on fire.

"Holly!" Dirk said, panicked.

From within the lift emerged a Mountain Dragon. He was larger, darker and scarier than Dirk. Grey smoke poured uncontrollably from his nose. Predatory eyes peered out from the smoke and a mouth curled into a sinister smile.

"Vainclaw Grandin," snarled Dirk.

"Dirk Dilly, dragon detective," replied the deep baritone voice.

"Whatever you're planning, it's over. I've got your henchmen bagged."

"Henchmen, yes... Not my hench-*dragons*,

though," replied Vainclaw.

From the lift behind him emerged Leon, the eldest of the two yellow-backed Scavenger brothers who worked for Vainclaw. He was holding a Sea Dragon, a claw jammed threateningly into her jaw.

"Delfina," said Alba desperately. "Are you all right?"

"Help me, sister. I fear for my life. They are maniacs," whimpered her sister. She looked terrified.

"Keep quiet, hard-back," growled Leon.

A second Scavenger climbed up through the hole Dirk had made in the lift and picked up what looked like a blood-stained bundle of clothes. As he stepped out on to the roof, Dirk could see that it was Mali, Leon's brother, and he was holding Holly, the blood from her leg smeared across his belly.

"All right, Mr Detective?" he said. "I've got your little friend here."

"If you hurt her I'll roast your heart, Mali," replied Dirk.

"You want me to chuck her over so we can have a fair fight?" replied the younger of the Scavenger brothers, holding Holly over the edge of the building.

"Not yet," snapped Leon.

"You never let me have any fun, bro," replied Mali.

"Cease your bickering," said Vainclaw. "We have work to do."

"Now, Mr Dilly, we are thirty-five floors above a hard concrete pavement," said Vainclaw Grandin, "so you will do everything I say otherwise my Scavenger will let go of the girl."

"Yeah, I'll give her a free flying lesson," said Mali, leaning forwards to dangle Holly over the side.

"There will be no tricks," said Vainclaw. "Is that clear?"

"Crystal clear," replied Dirk, through gritted teeth.

"I realized just after you'd gone," said Holly weakly. "GS doesn't stand for Global Sands—"

"Eh, who rattled your cage?" said Mali, shaking Holly, so that her bad leg flew about, causing her to cry out. Tears streamed down her face.

"GS stands for Gronkong Shinard." Vainclaw finished her sentence.

Dirk recognized the name. When he first discovered Kinghorns in London they had been hiding in a warehouse that was registered to a Gronkong Shinard.

"What is it?" he asked.

"Rearrange the letters to find our true identity."

It only took Dirk a moment to come up with the answer. "Kinghorn Dragons," he muttered. "But why would the Kinghorns have a company in the human world?"

"How naive you are," said Vainclaw. "Gronkong Shinard has been operating for a long, long time. Gronkong Shinard built this tower."

"This is a modern building," said Dirk. "It was built by humans."

"Humans employed by me," said Vainclaw. "They constructed it around a central stone spine built by dragons. Remember when our kind used to help these pathetic mammals to build their monuments in return for gold? The pyramids, Stonehenge, the Aztec temples, the Great Wall of China, all built with the help of dragons. But with this tower, Gronkong Shinard retained the rights to the top floor and roof. At the base of the foundations is an entrance that allows us to come and go as we please. So you see, our headquarters are in the heart of the human civilization that we will soon destroy." Vainclaw's sinister grin widened. "Now, Alba Longs, it is time for you to play your part."

"Please, no! I have told you how to be summoning a Sky Dragon. Why can you not let me go now and summon one for yourself?"

"You think I should spit fire into the belly of a Sky Dragon then politely ask that it joins me in my fight against humanity?" asked Vainclaw.

"So that's your plan," said Dirk. "The same as Karny, you want to summon a Sky Dragon."

Vainclaw turned to look at him, his eyes glowing. "Not just one Sky Dragon," he said. "I have been tracking the herd. They are flying over this city. When Alba spits the fire into the belly of the leader, it will materialize before us. I will say that humans are responsible for summoning them. I will explain that we Kinghorns are here to help them. Then the rest of the herd will materialize and the great war will begin. With the Skies, there will be no limit to our power."

"Please don't make me do it," begged Alba.

"She's innocent," said Dirk. "Do your own dirty work."

Vainclaw flared his nostrils. "Alba, you're off the hook. We have another volunteer."

"Me?" said Dirk. "Not a chance."

"Mali, show him what will happen if he does not obey," snarled Vainclaw.

Mali dangled Holly over the edge of the building.

"You wouldn't want me to drop her, would you?" said the yellow-backed Scavenger, letting her slide a little.

"Don't do it, Dirk!" Holly tried to sound brave but was unable to hide her fear.

"Don't hurt her!" shouted Dirk.

Mali stepped back from the edge and waited. Dirk took the flask from Alba and flipped the top open. Inside, the scorching liquid sizzled, bubbled and spat. The tiny sip he had taken at the Outer Core had been painful enough. In order to reach a Sky Dragon he would have to take a big gulp. It wasn't going to be fun.

"We don't have all night," said Vainclaw.

Dirk looked up at the overcast sky, bathed in the reflective glow of the city lights. He stared at the clouds, trying to distinguish a shape among them. It brought back a long-forgotten memory of being a very young dragon lying on a mountainside, looking up at the sky, trying to spot Sky Dragons.

"Hurry up," growled Vainclaw.

As Dirk's eyes adjusted to the dark, he saw that Vainclaw was right. There was no chance of rain that night in London. Upon closer inspection it was obvious that each cloud was shaped like a dragon. Some had been stretched and misshapen by the wind but they all had wings, tails and long, pointed noses. Some flew high, others much lower. The herd of Sky Dragons was drifting peacefully over the city but once they were summoned, they would form a formidable army for whichever side they chose.

"I see one above now," said Vainclaw. "Time is running out."

A bulbous dragon-shaped cloud was passing

directly overhead, its huge jaws wide open.

"Now!" ordered Vainclaw.

"No!" Holly cried.

"We're not joking about killing her," warned Leon.

Dirk understood that he faced the choice of preventing war or saving his friend, but there was no doubt in his mind as to the right course of action.

"Bottom's up," he said. Shutting his eyes in anticipation of the pain, he took a large swig from the flask. He tipped his head back and held the liquid fire in the back of his throat.

The pain tore through his body, scorching his insides. He screamed in agony and spat out the liquid fire. It shot up into the sky like a burning arrow but he had misjudged how quickly the Sky Dragon was moving. He missed. The jet of liquid fire rained down, splattering Vainclaw and the Scavengers. They shielded their eyes but otherwise seemed unconcerned by the scolding downpour. Dirk collapsed to his knees.

"What was that?" asked Mali, flicking a burning ember from his nose.

"Mr Detective missed the target," replied Leon.

"Try again," urged Vainclaw.

"Water," uttered Dirk, his throat as dry as a desert. The last thing he wanted to do was take another swig of the burning liquid, but he focused on Holly. He thought he could hear her saying something but the sounds around him were all blending into one.

"Summon the dragon or we drop the girl," said Vainclaw.

Dirk struggled back to his feet. Looking up, he saw another cloud dragon drifting overhead. Dirk lifted the flask to his lips and poured. The agony was excruciating. His vision was blurred but he steadied himself, took aim and spat the fire high into the sky.

This time, the liquid fire hit the Sky Dragon's wing. Bolts of white lightning zigzagged through the cloud.

Dirk dropped on to all fours, his head bowed. He couldn't speak but he heard Vainclaw's distinctive baritone say, "If you don't get it next time, we will decorate the pavement with your friend."

Dirk lifted himself back to his feet with his last bit of energy and checked the flask. There was only enough left for one more attempt and the cloud was almost out of range. He had to move fast. He took the final gulp of liquid fire, charged forwards, leaped, then spat the orange liquid at the dragon.

"Aghhhh yeahh!" he roared as the fire hit the target. The cloud fizzed, sizzled, hissed and cracked as the molecules of gas transformed into solid living flesh.

"Kinghorns, prepare!" ordered Vainclaw.

The Sky Dragon crashed down on to the top of the skyscraper, its soft wispy edges hardening and revealing a dragon three times bigger even than Vainclaw himself. Its back was sky blue, its belly cloud-white. Its eyes burned like the summer sun and its wings were the size of ship sails. It clasped a yellow claw to its heart in agony, then dropped on to its belly, shaking the building to its foundations.

Dirk gasped for breath. He could barely speak but he managed to mutter "I'm sorry," before he passed out altogether.

25

"Nooo!"

Holly cried out in despair and agony. She had watched Dirk being tortured, broken and defeated, all for her sake.

"Oi, little girl, keep a lid on it," said Mali, his stinking breath warming her face. He spun round and held her over the edge. She looked down at the Londoners in the streets below, oblivious to the drama unfolding on top of the skyscraper. It was a long way to fall.

"But I need to help him," she whispered.

Mali swung back to face the others but Holly's view of Dirk was obscured by the collapsed Sky Dragon. As magnificent as it was, the dragon was in a sorry state. In the centre of its blue back was a black burn mark, where the liquid fire had torn through its body. It coughed and a cloud of ash flew off its skin, landing on the ground, producing a perfect outline of its body. The Sky Dragon raised its enormous head wearily and looked at Holly. Its eyes that had burned so brightly were now creamy white, revealing the poor animal's obvious pain.

Vainclaw stepped forwards and bowed respectfully.

"Sky Dragon, I, Vainclaw Grandin, greet you. I am sorry we were too slow to prevent the humans from summoning you. What is your name?"

"My name is Nebula Colorado," replied a female voice as soft and warm as a summer's breeze. "It was a dragon who did this."

"Yes, this dragon traitor works with humans," said Vainclaw, pointing at Dirk. "They summoned you so that they might kill you. We raced as fast as we could to stop them but we were too late."

"It's not true!" shouted Holly with all the energy she could muster. "Don't listen to—"

Mali clasped a clammy paw over her mouth, preventing her from speaking.

"Nebula, you must summon the herd." Vainclaw's words dripped like poison. "The humans are planning to attack. You have stayed in the sky too long. It is time to return and join us to defeat them."

The Sky Dragon tipped her head back and blew, sending a swirling tornado of smoke into the air. "It is done. I have called the Skies. They are coming." Nebula shut her eyes and slumped to the floor.

Vainclaw inspected the body. "She's out," he announced.

Dirk? What can we do? Holly thought hard, remembering how he had spoken in her head when they had been up against the Kinghorns the last time. There was no response.

Vainclaw turned to Holly, smoke pouring from his nose. "I imagine you're waiting for your detective to save the day," he said.

Holly tried to answer but the words came out as a painful cough.

"Alba Longs, check on Mr Dilly," ordered Vainclaw. "Do it quickly or Leon will slice up your sister."

"They mean what they say," said Delfina, her voice quivering with fear.

"That's right. I'll cut up your sister and feed her to the pigeons." Leon dug his claw further into Delfina's chin.

Shaking with every step, Alba made her way around the Sky Dragon. "Mr Dirk is still here," she said. "There is no movement from him at all."

"You see, little girl?" said Vainclaw to Holly. "We've won. All we have to do now is wait for the other Sky Dragons to appear then we will take our new allies straight down to the Outer Core to build up their strength ready for the beginning of the war. Dragons against humans. And we'll win because we will be united. All dragons, under one sky."

"Er, boss…" said Mali, sounding nervous. "Won't the humans notice all them Skies appearing over the city?"

"Who cares?" snapped Vainclaw, with a dismissive wave. "The time is upon us. We have waited too long for this. Finally, we will have the ultimate weapons… Sky Dragons. With the Skies on our side, all of dragonkind will join us. Then we will pluck humans from their position of power. Once we have won they will bow down to dragons. Kinghorns will rule them all and I, Vainclaw Grandin, the first up-airer, shall rule the world!" Vainclaw shouted triumphantly.

"Nice speech, boss," said Leon.

"Yeah, it was really stirring," Mali said enthusiastically.

"It won't work," said Holly weakly.

Vainclaw looked at her with an amused smile. "What would you know, a mere human child?"

"You won't be able to trick the Sky Dragons. They won't join you," said Holly stubbornly.

"Shall I drop her, boss?" said Mali, dangling Holly over the edge again.

Vainclaw brought his face close to hers, pungent smoke blowing from his nostrils. He extended a claw and pushed it into Holly's cheek.

"So soft. So vulnerable." He smiled. "Yes, drop her."

Holly felt Mali's grip loosen.

He let go and she fell.

Karnataka would have happily ignored Dirk's fire flare but Archie saw it too. "That means they've found the truck, doesn't it?" he said.

"Maybe," mumbled Karnataka.

"It does. Come on. We have to help them," said Archie, who had noticed that Karnataka hadn't exactly been searching very hard for the truck.

"Why?" demanded Karny.

"Because Holly is my friend," replied Archie resolutely. "And because this is all way too much fun to give up on now. Oh, and I think there was something about saving the world."

They came to a rest on top of a bakery with air vents churning out delicious smells. Karnataka craned his head round to look at Archie. "No."

"Scaredy-cat," goaded Archie.

"I'm not a cat and I'm not scared. Just naturally cautious," replied Karnataka in his high-pitched whine, pacing around an air vent.

"Oh, well, you won't mind if you get seen, then will you?" said Archie, placing two fingers in his mouth and whistling to attract some attention.

"Quiet! Stop it!" said Karnataka, stepping away from the edge.

"Only if you take me to the others."

"I hate humans," Karnataka grumbled, but he turned and headed towards the Thames where the flare had come from.

After they crossed the river, the trail went cold. No more flares went up and they couldn't find any trace of the reddish-coloured truck. Karnataka was prepared to give up but then Archie spotted an orange streak in the sky, above a skyscraper in central London.

Karnataka landed on a low roof near the building, above a bar playing loud electronic music. He could feel the bass beneath his feet. The clink of glasses and hum of human chatter rose up into the warm night air.

"We should go up," Archie said.

"This is close enough," replied Karnataka.

A second streak of light appeared above the tall building, then a third. Something was happening but it was too high up to see what.

"It looks like the sky is going to collapse," said Archie.

"It's this kind of thing that makes us Shade-Huggers prefer to stay underground," said Karnataka.

They continued to watch. Something was being dangled over the edge of the building.

"What's that?" exclaimed Archie.

A scream cut through the air.

"It's Holly! Go!"

Karnataka was surprised both by the way Archie kicked his heels into his belly and by the way he understood the command and obeyed. He spread his wings and flew up towards the falling girl.

"Hold tight," he yelled to Archie as he swivelled upside down, causing the boy to dangle precariously from his neck. There was a jolt and Archie almost lost his grip as Holly landed on the Shade-Hugger's soft underbelly. Karnataka clamped a foreleg over the girl, holding her safely in place, then turned and flew upwards.

Hurtling up the side of the building, Holly and Archie found themselves face to face over Karnataka's shoulder.

"Good timing," said Holly weakly.

"What's wrong?" asked Archie.

"My leg's broken, Dirk's passed out and the Kinghorns have the Sky Dragons on their side."

"Kinghorns, you say?" Karnataka quickly changed direction and began to fly back down.

"What are you doing?" said Holly and Archie together.

"When it comes to fight or flight, I'm more of a flight dragon," said Karnataka.

"There ... won't be anywhere to hide once ... the war begins," said Holly, agony in every syllable.

Karnataka knew they were right. "You're really starting to bug me," he said, reluctantly changing direction again and flying back up the side of the building towards the top, zooming past the floors of empty offices.

27

On the roof, Mali was looking down. "It's the Shade-Hugger, the one that took your captain job, bro. He's rescued the girl and he's got another kid. Let me at him!"

"No," said Vainclaw firmly. "Allow him to land. From all I hear about this Captain Karnataka it will be easy enough to persuade him to switch sides."

Karnataka landed on his hind legs next to Dirk's unconscious body. Archie slid off his back, then Karnataka laid Holly gently down beside Dirk.

"Di-Dirk?" Holly put her hand to his face. Dirk said nothing. Holly rested her head on his cheek and closed her eyes.

"How exquisitely pathetic," said Vainclaw.

"Welcome, Captain Karnataka. Firstly, let me congratulate you on this marvellous Sky Dragon plan. How inventive you are."

"Mr Captain Karnataka, sir," said Alba. "You did lie to me—"

"Keep quiet, Sea Dragon," said Leon. "Else I'll cut your sister's throat."

"I do not think he is fooling," said Delfina.

"Enough!" barked Vainclaw. "Shade-Hugger, I'm going to come straight to the point. I have a proposal. Shortly, the rest of the Sky Dragons will appear. Look – they are already gathering."

Karnataka looked up. The edge of the purple sky was blackening as though a storm was closing in from all sides. The Sky Dragon herd was nearing.

"I'll give you one chance," continued Vainclaw. "Join us now and you can be one of us. The Kinghorns always have time for a dragon of your moral flexibility."

Karnataka glanced at Archie.

"You can't do it," the boy said.

"Sorry." Karnataka shrugged. "Like I always say ... cowards survive." He walked towards Vainclaw, edging around the unconscious Sky Dragon. "You've got yourself a deal," he said.

"I knew you were my kind of dragon," said Vainclaw.

Desperate, Archie turned to Holly but she was lying still, passed out in pain, oblivious to her surroundings. Archie leaned over her and whispered in Dirk's ear. "What can I do?"

For a moment there was nothing. Then a tiny puff of smoke drifted up from Dirk's nostrils.

"What are you trying to tell me?" repeated Archie.

The smoke formed three distinct shapes. Three letters that only lasted a moment, but long enough for Archie to read the word SKY.

Archie looked up. The storm of dragons grew closer. Dirk's smoke formed an arrow, pointing to the large unconscious dragon in the centre of the roof.

"Kinghorns, prepare," said Vainclaw. "When they arrive, we shall terminate these humans to show our Sky Dragon allies that the war has begun."

Archie snuck past the unconscious crooks in the net then around the Sky Dragon's large body, crawling through the thick line of ash that surrounded it.

"Hey, er, Sky Dragon," he whispered in Nebula's

huge velvety ear. "Look, I don't know what your name is … or if you can understand me … or if you're even alive … but the point is, you have to wake up."

Nothing.

Archie tried to lift one of Nebula's huge eyelids up but it was locked shut. He was about to give up when the corner of the dragon's mouth moved.

"Too … weak," muttered the dragon. "Need what you call … su-garrr."

"Sugar?" said Archie.

The black cloud army continued to close in on them. Leon released Delfina and stood threateningly over Arthur and Reg. Mali joined him, both Scavengers ready to kill them when Vainclaw gave the word.

"Delfina? Are you hurt?" said Alba.

Before Alba's sister could respond, Karnataka sprang forwards and kicked Mali in the ear. He whacked Leon with his tail, before landing on top of Vainclaw and pinning him down with his claws. "Alba and Delfina, get the Scavengers!" he cried.

"Betray me, would you?" snarled Vainclaw.

"I'm still the captain of the Dragnet and you are under arrest," said Karnataka.

"Release him." The voice spoke in his ear. Karnataka felt a claw around his throat.

"Delfina?" said Alba in surprise. "What are you doing? Captain Karnataka is on our side!"

Delfina forced Karnataka off Vainclaw, her sharp claws pressed against his neck. "You're wrong, sister," she said. "I am on the same side as my leader, Vainclaw Grandin."

"You… You are… You are a *Kinghorn*?" stammered Alba in disbelief.

"I was spying for Vainclaw when that stupid Drake arrested me." Delfina laughed. "You see, sometimes they get it right. I was the one who told Vainclaw of Karnataka's plan to contact the Skies."

"Next time I put you in prison I'm throwing away the key," said Karnataka.

Delfina pushed a claw into his ribs.

Above, the dark dragon clouds were beginning to swoop down. In the streets below the humans ran for cover, fearing a storm. But no rain fell. Instead, the sky began to bubble and sizzle, as though the clouds had been set alight.

"What a shame, Captain Karnataka," said Vainclaw

Grandin. "You're about to watch the dawn of a new era and you've just blown your chance of being a part of it."

Then another voice spoke, drifting through the air like a gust of wind.

"It's too early for dawn," spoke Nebula. "The night has just begun."

Vainclaw spun around to see the huge Sky Dragon looming over him, standing on her hind legs, head raised to the sky. Her pale blue back darkened to match the sky behind her. Archie stood in front of this magnificent beast and tossed a jelly bean into the air. Nebula ducked down and snatched it between her jaws.

"Sky Dragon... Nebula... Friend," Vainclaw spoke slowly, emphasizing each word. "It is heartening to see you have regained your strength so speedily. Now we must join forces and strike against these human aggressors."

The Sky Dragon glanced at the unconscious human crooks before turning her cloud-white eyes back to Vainclaw.

"You lied to me," she said.

"The Skies must join the Kinghorns," growled Vainclaw.

"We will not join you. The herd will not materialize," said Nebula.

Vainclaw Grandin looked up to see that the Sky

Dragons were now retreating. His eyes narrowed and the smoke from his nostrils darkened. "If you won't join us, step aside so we can rid ourselves of this incompetent captain and that interfering detective."

"You will harm no one." Nebula spread her wings to block his way.

"I've always liked Sky Dragons. Never met one before, mind, but I definitely like you," babbled Karnataka nervously, edging behind Nebula's wing. "Good to know you're on our side."

"The Skies have no sides," she said. "We stand with none but our own."

"But he wants to start a war!" protested Karnataka.

"And you want to stop it," she replied patiently. "Yes, we do understand. We just don't care. We have no interest in such matters. Sky Dragons exist simply and simply exist. Gaze up at us if you like but we are beyond your reach. We are the oldest of all creatures and, as long as there is wind, we shall outlive you all."

Vainclaw growled, black smoke billowing from his nose. "We will see about that."

Delfina and the Scavenger brothers moved swiftly into attack formation, heads lowered, claws drawn, jaws open. Vainclaw moved slowly but purposefully, keeping watch on Nebula. Karnataka edged back, stepping on Dirk's tail, causing him to let out a low groan. Alba looked back and forth between the Kinghorns and the Sky Dragon, unsure what to do.

"It is time for you to pick a side as well, sister," said Delfina. "Join us or betray your kind."

Alba looked into her sister's yellow eyes with renewed anger. "You are no sister of mine," she spat. She moved next to Nebula, quivering with every step. "I am not scared. I will fight."

"Stand behind me, Sea Dragon," said Nebula calmly.

"OK," said Alba. As she took cover behind Nebula's enormous wing, she stood on Dirk's paw. He let out another moan. "Very sorry, Mr Dirk," she said.

"Let's see what this Sky Dragon has got then," jeered Leon.

"Yeah, give us your best shot," goaded Mali.

Nebula opened her mouth and swung her head around, making an awful rasping noise, but no flames came out.

"She's got no fire!" cackled Mali.

Holly stirred. "What's going on?" she asked weakly, opening her eyes for a moment.

"I don't think she's got any fire," said Archie.

"It's toasting time, Sky Dragon," said Leon.

"You should have joined us when you had the chance," said Vainclaw.

"Let's set the Sky on fire!" added Mali.

"Set this guy on fire?" said Leon.

"The *Sky* not *this guy*," said Delfina.

"We have the flames of four dragons," said Vainclaw. "Nothing – no matter how powerful – can survive that."

As one, the Kinghorns sent four powerful jets of fire at Nebula. Archie shielded Holly from the heat. He felt as though his back was being cooked but when he looked up, he saw that the flames had been stopped.

The Kinghorns stood, furious and confused, behind a wall of fire twenty metres high.

"Leon, fly over it!" ordered Vainclaw.

Leon shot into the sky but as he tried to get over the firewall, Nebula waved a paw, sending a ball of fire into his chin. The smell of burning dragon flesh filled the air and Leon tumbled back down, still on the same side of the wall.

"Hey, bro, you've burned your nose," laughed Mali.

"You two, go around it," demanded Vainclaw, pointing at Mali and Delfina.

They took a side each but, this time, Nebula moved both paws, causing giant flames to shoot out in both directions, scorching their wings and sending them back to where they had started.

"Oi, Mali," said Leon, "you've burned your wing."

"Shut your mouth."

"You shut yours!"

"Both of you, be quiet." Vainclaw paced back and forth, inspecting the strange phenomenon. "It's burning away. Once it has gone, we will take her apart without fire. We will use our teeth and our claws."

Nebula opened her jaws and breathed more flame into the firewall. It curled round at the edges, encircling and entrapping the Kinghorns.

"Leave," she said.

"You don't need to ask me twice." Mali flew upwards, only to find that the circle of fire became a dome. He crashed down into his brother.

"Not up," said Nebula. "Down."

"She is too powerful," noted Delfina.

"Sorry, boss," said Leon. "Come on, bro."

Leon, Mali and Delfina slipped through the doorway that led to the elevator shaft.

"Cowards!" Vainclaw stood upright and stared furiously at Nebula through the flames. He spread his wings, one of which was torn and frayed at the edge. He opened his mouth but Nebula cut him off before he could make a sound.

"Your Dragonsong is no use here. We Skies can direct the wind. We hear what we want to hear."

Vainclaw growled, frustrated but finally understanding that he was defeated. "When the war comes..." He spoke in a measured tone. "Then we will show no mercy to your kind. Mark my words, when this human world is aflame with our fire, we will torch the Skies as well."

With these final words, he turned and fled.

With the Kinghorns gone, Nebula blinked and the firewall burned away to nothing. Archie clapped and whooped, then said, "I have seen some cool things today but a bunch of evil dragons imprisoned inside a dome of fire, that takes the biscuit."

"You are hard to understand, human," said Nebula. "But I am grateful for the sustenance. I haven't tasted sugar since the Middle Ages. It's better than I remember."

Archie found another jelly bean in his pocket and held it out for Nebula. She nibbled it off his hand.

"Did we win?" uttered a small, pained voice.

Holly was lying against Dirk, her leg mangled, her jeans drenched in fresh blood, agony in her eyes.

"Gather up the ash," Nebula commanded Archie and Alba, taking in Holly's injuries. "Stay away from the edge. Humans may still be looking."

"I hope they do not see Mr Captain Karnataka then," said Alba.

Archie and Nebula looked up to see the Shade-Hugger flying fast up into the sky, his dark brown back quickly vanishing into the night.

"Never mind him, bring the ash here and cover the wound," ordered Nebula. She tore Holly's jeans to expose her bloody and bruised leg.

Archie carried a handful of fine ash over to Holly and sprinkled it on to her leg. She gritted her teeth in pain.

"Sorry, Holly," he said.

"Now cover the rest of leg," ordered Nebula.

Archie brought more until the whole leg was covered with ash.

"Stand back." Nebula opened her mouth and breathed blue flames, which licked over the ash.

Holly cried out in pain again.

"You're hurting her!" said Archie, trying to pull Nebula away.

"No, she is being made all the better. Look." Alba

pointed to Holly's leg. The ash turned golden under the blue flame and the spilled blood was drawn back into her leg.

Nebula closed her mouth and the flames vanished. "The bone is fixed," she said.

The leg still looked bruised and raw but the wound had been sealed. With Archie's help, Holly tried to stand. Tentatively, she put some weight on to the leg. She looked up in amazement. "It's better," she said. "How did you do that?"

"Dragon or human, skin or bone, we all need the same things to survive: water, earth, air and fire. It takes fire to mend a broken bone," said Nebula.

Holly turned to Archie. "That's the second time you've saved my life."

"The dragons did all the hard work." He grinned. Then, eyes widening, he added, "*Dragons*, Holly. I can't believe it. I knew you were worth following. I knew it."

"Now, let's see about the one who summoned me." Nebula bent down to inspect Dirk, who still hadn't moved since swallowing the liquid fire.

"It wasn't his fault," said Holly.

"I know," said Nebula.

"Will he be all right?"

"He needs water. Sea Dragon, hold his mouth open," said Nebula, then she raised her head to the sky and took a long intake of breath.

Alba lifted Dirk's head and prised his jaws open. Holly and Archie watched as a strand of vaporized water fell from a cloud above. Nebula caught it, allowing it to run through her paws and trickle into Dirk's open mouth as pure, cool, fresh water.

"How is she doing that?" asked Archie.

"I *think* she's milking a cloud," replied Holly.

Dirk coughed and spluttered, then his eyes opened and he sat up.

"Dirk, you're alright!" Holly threw her arms around him.

"Hey, kiddo," he replied, smiling.

"I'm sorry, Mr Dirk. I am sorry I deceived you," said Alba, head bowed. "I just wanted to save Delfina but now I know that it is too late for her."

"I've met a fair few deceitful dragons in my time." Dirk lifted her head with the curve of his claw. "I'm not counting you as one of them. You did what was necessary to protect your sister. Even if you couldn't protect her from herself."

"Thank you," said Alba. "I don't know how to repay you."

"The standard method is to actually pay me," replied Dirk. "But seeing as we've just prevented the war to end all wars, let's call it quits."

"And what about you and I?" asked Nebula. "Shall we call it quits?"

"I'm sorry," said Dirk. "I had no choice."

"No choice but to start a war?"

"No choice but to save a friend."

"These are complicated times I have materialized into," she said. "Dragons are divided. Humans are more powerful than ever. Decisions get harder in times like these. I didn't get your name and I don't even know the name of this remarkable citadel."

"The name is Dirk Dilly, dragon detective. And you're standing in the middle of the city of London. It's not the largest human city in the world, nor the oldest. It's definitely not the happiest, but in the opinion of this old fire-breather, it's the greatest."

"I am not so keen," said Alba.

"It's not for everyone," admitted Dirk. "Now, take Nebula down to the core. She will need to recover. These crooks will wake up soon and we shouldn't be here when they do." Dirk indicated the net where Arthur and Reg lay unconscious. "Holly, Archie, it's time to say farewell."

Archie had never been one for long, drawn-out goodbyes. He didn't see the point when relatives made a big fuss after they had been to stay, but saying goodbye to Alba and Nebula was different. Two real-life dragons, as majestic and magnificent as he could ever have imagined, were looking at him, not just to say goodbye but to thank him for helping them. He could see the tears running down Holly's face as she hugged Alba. He cried too.

Dirk had taken Archie home first, then delivered Holly to her room. After a long hug, he had lowered his tail, allowing her to climb through her bedroom window. She landed with a thud.

"Holly?" yelled Mr Bigsby.

There were footsteps on the stairs followed by more shouting.

"Where have you been? We've been worried sick! What time do you call this? Why are your jeans torn? What a state! You look like you've been to war."

Holly's response was too quiet for Dirk to hear but he could detect her tone. It was stubborn, determined and strong. It was Holly.

The next day she had phoned. "They're having steel

bars put on the window," she said.

"Steel's no problem," replied Dirk, snapping his jaws together.

"They'll get really suspicious if you break the bars. No, I'm stuck here for the whole holiday." Holly tried not to sound too glum. "It was worth it, though. We stopped Vainclaw and we stole the instructions for that volcano weapon from Buchanan."

"I'm just relieved he doesn't know about dragons," said Dirk. "Fighting Kinghorns is one thing but if a human as rich and powerful as Buchanan knew the truth about us, life would get very complicated."

Once he had hung up, Dirk left the office and went back to work. After all, he still had a case open. He sat on the roof across the road from the small art gallery. The doubled-chinned security guard was fast asleep in front of the screens, snoring, with his hand inside a doughnut box.

While he waited, Dirk went back to his book.

As no one knows for sure whether Sky Dragons really can create firewalls, no one knows how they work. One theory popular among cryptozoologists, however, is that Sky Dragons can separate air particles and, in the instance of the firewall, isolate the oxygen. As pure oxygen is flammable, it only takes a flame to ignite it and for that section of the air to become a burning wall of fire. This would also explain other powers sometimes attributed to Sky Dragons, such as the ability to draw water particles from clouds and to deflect harmful sounds away, such as Dragonsong.

Dirk looked up from the book to find that the row of security cameras had gone fuzzy. He checked the street below and flew to the large window, which he pushed open before climbing into the gallery. This time, he was prepared and held one paw over his nose to stop the trail of smoke from triggering the alarm.

Looking around the room, he spotted a camera neutralizer in the corner of the gallery. On the floor was the painting of the sad-looking lady. It was moving exactly as before but this time it was heading back towards the spot where it had originally hung. The picture was being returned.

Dirk stooped down and lifted up the moving

painting. Underneath were six white mice. They had metallic collars around their necks and tiny mechanical devices on their backs. Four of them were equipped with electronic clips that were allowing them to carry the stolen picture. One had a glasscutter. Dirk picked up another and inspected the grappling hook it was carrying. *So that's how they got the picture down from the wall*, he thought. The mouse between his paws didn't struggle. Dirk would have thought them mechanical were it not for the tiny heartbeat he could feel.

He looked more closely at the device on its back and saw, in very small lettering, a G and an S etched in a circle.

Dirk was so stunned to see the Global Sands logo that he forgot to keep his paw over his nose. A thin line of grey smoke escaped from his right nostril and drifted up through the room, into the vent in a small white box on the ceiling, setting off the fire alarm.

"Sweet rats from Sweden! Not again..." He dropped the mouse, scampered across the room and leaped out of the window before the security guard came charging into the gallery.

The next morning Dirk phoned the gallery and asked for Mr Strettingdon-Smythe.

"Ah, Mr Dilly," said the plumy-voiced curator. "I was just going to call you. You'll never guess what has happened."

"One of the stolen paintings has been returned?" he ventured.

"Oh, you did guess," said Mr Strettingdon-Smythe. "Yes, the *Sad-Looking Lady* was returned last night. It's very peculiar. Can you understand it?"

"I'm beginning to get the picture," said Dirk, inwardly groaning at his own pun. "When you called me you said your boss didn't want you to contact anyone."

"That's right. He said it would be bad for business."

"And may I ask the name of your boss?" Dirk asked, pouring himself a glass of neat orange squash.

"The gallery is owned by Global Sands. Brant Buchanan himself forbade me from calling anyone."

Dirk knocked the orange squash back in one. "My advice to you would be to wait. In time, all the paintings will be returned."

"But what's going on?" Mr Strettingdon-Smythe barked.

"It's safer for you if you don't know," said Dirk firmly.

It was clear to him now that Buchanan was using the art gallery as a training ground for his mouse thieves. That's why he wouldn't allow the curator to call the police. He was stealing from himself. The metallic collars the mice wore must have enabled him to control them remotely, turning them into unwitting mini criminals. Mice could get in anywhere and with enough of them they could steal anything from a painting to a secret government weapon.

"Have a good day, Mr Strettingdon-Smythe." Dirk put the phone down and switched on the morning news.

"After days of speculation regarding the strange sightings on top of a London skyscraper last Tuesday, the mystery has finally been solved," the newsreader was saying. "A spokesperson for Gronkong Shinard PLC, the company that owns the top floor and roof of the building, explained that they had been testing new weather-predicting equipment at the time."

Dirk sat back and bit open a tin of beans.

"And now back to our main story," continued the newsreader. "Volcanologists are struggling to explain why three volcanoes, thought to be dormant, have erupted simultaneously and unexpectedly." Images of flowing lava and ash clouds filled the screen. "In a strange coincidence, all three volcanoes were situated on islands owned by Brant Buchanan, the seventh richest man in the world. Although no one was hurt in the eruptions, the islands have suffered severe damage and the surrounding air space has been deemed a no-fly zone. Mr Buchanan was unavailable for comment."

In another part of London, in the back of his Bentley, Brant Buchanan was also watching the news report, laughing, clapping his hands together.

"How are the share prices, Weaver?" he asked.

Weaver's face appeared on the plasma screen. "It looks like it's worked, sir," he said. "The insurance payout for the three islands is so big that the share prices for the insurance company are plummeting, meaning you can buy the company at a bargain price."

Sensing the disapproval in his employee's voice, Buchanan said, "You think it's extravagant to erupt three volcanoes in order to buy an insurance company on the cheap, don't you, Weaver?"

"I think some would call it extravagant," replied the driver, choosing his words carefully.

"What would *you* call it?"

"I'd call it a rich man's hobby," he said.

"It's lucky you made a copy of the instructions," said Buchanan. "Talking of which, let's have a look at that security video."

The image of Weaver's face slid to the side of the screen and grainy CCTV footage appeared showing three angles of the upstairs office in the lab. Across the bottom of the screen ran the time.

19:46:58

19:46:59

At 19:47:00 something about the size of a golf ball dropped into the room.

"It was rather bold of these thieves to use our own

215

camera-neutralizer to break into the office," said Buchanan.

"Luckily, as it was our own equipment I was able to isolate the scrambling frequency and recover the picture," said Weaver. "The thief should be entering any second."

Surprise was not something Brant Buchanan often experienced. He wasn't surprised when Mrs Bigsby had told him the location of the VE 6.2 in exchange for a good job with a generous salary. He wasn't surprised that Weaver's remote-controlled mice had successfully stolen the weapon. He wasn't surprised when the weapon actually worked, erupting the volcanoes and enabling him to make even more money.

But his jaw dropped as he watched the CCTV footage. From three different angles, he saw a real, live dragon drop into the office. The dragon glanced around, surveying the room. Weaver paused the footage on a close-up of the creature's large face. It stared directly into the camera. An actual dragon. In spite of his childhood fantasies, Brant Buchanan had never dreamed that dragons actually existed, let alone that one could break into his office. But there it was in front of him. Evidence.

The billionaire leaned forwards to get a closer look. "What have we here?" he uttered.

"I'd say you have a new hobby," replied Weaver drily.

Out Now:

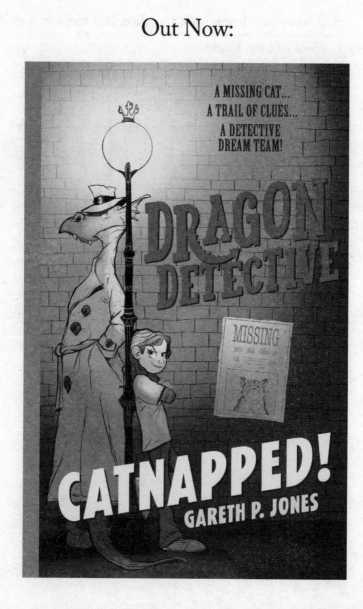

A MISSING CAT...
A TRAIL OF CLUES...
A DETECTIVE DREAM TEAM!

DRAGON DETECTIVE

MISSING

CATNAPPED!

GARETH P. JONES

Out Now:

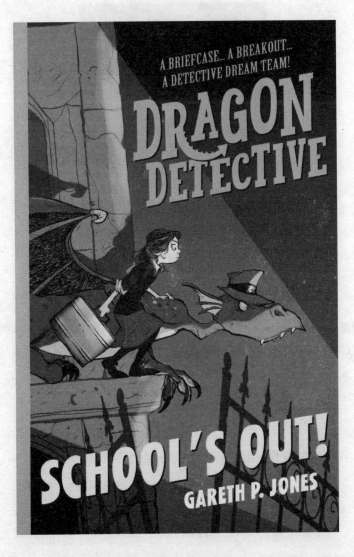

About the Author

Gareth P. Jones is a Blue Peter Award-winning children's author of over 40 books for children of all ages, including *The Thornthwaite Inheritance*, *The Considine Curse* and *Death or Ice Cream*. His series fiction includes Ninja Meerkats, Adventures of the Steampunk Pirates, Pet Defenders and Dragon Detective.

Gareth regularly visits schools all over the world as well as performing at festivals. He plays ukulele, trumpet, guitar, accordion and piano to varying levels of incompetence. He lives in south-east London with his wife and two children.